Bedtim

for Kids

*A Collection of the Best Animals,
Dinosaurs, Unicorns, Dragons
Adventures Tales to Help Children to
Fall Asleep Fast at Night and Feel
Calm Having Beautiful Dreams*

Oliver King

Table of Contents

Conclusion

Introduction

Congratulations on your purchase of *Bedtime Stories for Kids*, and thank you so much for choosing this title to inspire the creativity of your little ones. This time, in a child's life, is full of wonder and mystery. When you are processing new information all the time, everything seems profound and magical. It is up to us to encourage that imagination.

Reading to your child can allow you to channel their creativity in a healthy and exciting way. You can be the guide that ushers your little one away to magical lands. Introduce them to characters that they will fall in love with. You can control the content that they are consuming while also adventuring right alongside them.

Bedtime stories are a tried and true method of relaxation at the end of a stimulating day.

Studies have shown that children benefit from having a routine before they sleep. This can be time that you use to train your little one's brain to unwind so that they are able to find rest, even after the most chaotic days.

Each of these tales was written to teach the morals and values that you are already working to instill in your children. The easiest way to learn is through entertainment. As the parent, you can pass on these lessons without your child even realizing that they are being taught. There is so much imaginative children's literature on the market. Thank you again for choosing this book, and I hope that it offers a lot of joy to you and your little one.

Chapter 1: Unlikely Friends

Missy was a common field mouse. As she began to grow and the fur began to emerge from her tiny pink body, her parents noticed something strange. Right upon her chest was the outline of a heart, deep brown in color.

The strange pattern in her fur, made her stand out from the other mice. Everyone around her was a chestnut color, and they all had white bellies. Missy had a chocolate heart stamped upon her, front-and-center.

When she was very young, she did not like looking different from her peers. Missy would have given anything to not have the strange brown blob on her fur. Everyone around her looked so perfect and uniform. The young mouse became quite tired of explaining the abnormality to new animals who ventured into the mouse community.

The younger mice around her did not seem to appreciate her coat; the way her parents did. They all made fun of Missy, teasing her for looking different. She always felt like the odd-mouse-out. She would sit alone in class and doodle in the dirt around her.

Missy's confidence was nonexistent during those dark days. The little mouse just could not understand that she was special, and that variation was necessary for nature. Life would have been so boring if every flower bloomed the same. Imagine if every tree rustled their leaves in the wind in the same way. New shapes and colors added value to the scenery; they did not take away.

The mouse community lived in a vast valley below a stoic rocky mountain range. Their land was an oasis for small mammals. They all lazed about in tall grass beneath clear blue skies and ample sunlight. So many bird's pleasant songs rang out through the forest behind their field, creating a sweet soundtrack to the bright days.

During the spring, the field would smell of honeysuckle. When the mice were not in school or going about their various jobs, they played in the soft light of pastel sunsets. Missy liked to watch the brilliant colors as they swirled in the sky above her. The young mouse had taken an interest in the heavens and especially adored watching the stars. Such displays made her feel so small, in comparison.

Missy had heard that other mouse communities lived in fear. There was always some predator or another after their families. She'd heard stories of these mice having to live a life on the run from the next big thing with sharp teeth.

This was not something that her community ever worried about. She believed they must have found the perfect home because no animal or large bird had ever bothered them. The grass in the field was too tall to see beyond. The mice were too fast to catch, anyway. Life was relaxing. One year, everything changed.

There was no animal that threatened their livelihood; it was mother nature, herself. One year, when spring came, so did the rains. When the rain fell onto their field, the mice would retreat to a nearby cave in the forest. It was large enough to harbor their whole community. Other animals shared this shelter, each forgiving their natural grudges for the length of the bad weather.

Missy had always looked forward to the rain. She loved shifts in weather, and she loved hiding in the cave. She once sat beside a beautiful raccoon, whom she found fascinating. Opossums had some of the most interesting stories and were usually willing to humor the young mouse with the heart upon her chest.

As they all sat in the cave, during that fateful spring, the animals watched as the water began to rise. The forest had never flooded before; it had never even been close. None of the hiding animals had even considered the possibility that their cave could ever flood. The rain just would not stop falling.

There was a panic radiating slowly through the crowd of woodland creatures. The mice watched on, worried about their own land. There was still some time before the water reached their cave, but it was evident that flooding was a possibility.

"Someone is going to have to search for higher ground. Maybe in the mountains?" Said a chipmunk. Missy could not help but admire the two white racing stripes covering the length of his small back.

"We can't go into the mountains. There are dangers that lurk within those hills, and none of us are willing to sacrifice ourselves," said the beautiful raccoon.

"We are sacrificing ourselves if we stay here and wait for the water to swallow us," said an owl, perched in the shadows.

"Easy for you to say, you can fly!" Said a mouse.

"Yes, I can fly, but what will I eat if the land is taken over by water?"

"It can be you who searches for higher land, then," said the opossum.

"I will not venture into the mountains. I will give one of you a ride to the mountains, and you can do it," the owl replied, flatly. Missy could tell that he was afraid.

"The mice can draw straws!" Proclaimed the raccoon. There was a commotion all around the room. All of the animals argued about his idea. There was an intense back-and-forth as they all bargained for their own safety. Finally, it was agreed. The mice would all draw straws, and the loser would go to the mountains to locate a safe hideout for the duration of the floods.

"Don't worry! You will be hailed as a hero upon your safe return! We will find a way to thank you!" Said the raccoon. He was seemingly speaking into the ether, as he held a fist-full of straw toward each mouse. Missy knew immediately that she had lost.

The young mouse didn't say a word as she watched everyone around her, pulling longer straws. Her father saw her face and attempted to snatch the short stick from her. He wanted to trade before any of the other animals noticed. Missy held tight to her fate; she would not allow her father to make the journey on her behalf. She loved her parents too much to sacrifice them to the mountains.

"It is I! I have the shortest stick! I will make this journey!" Missy exclaimed. The raccoon looked at her with confusion in his face. They had not even passed out the other bits of straw, yet. He was halfway through the nervous mice. The young mouse wanted to make sure that her parents didn't try to take her stick; she was willing to risk being wrong about being the loser.

The owl was careful with the young mouse, on their flight to the bottom of the mountain. They flew through treacherous rain. Missy found herself hiding beneath the fluffy feathers on the owl's back, which kept her warm and dry for the most part.

Being in the air was a new experience for the little mouse. She held on to the owl's feathers with all available limbs. They designated a time to meet up (in three days' time) and a location, which happened to be a large boulder.

Missy trekked through the thick mud and horrible weather for hours. The young mouse thought that she might never get a break from the onslaught of water draining from the heavens. She ran from rock to the rock, tree to tree.

The night began to fall when it finally registered to the young mouse that she was in danger. Missy was in a foreign place with no experience and no friends. She regretted the eagerness with which she took the assignment, for a moment.

That is when the little mouse heard the screech. The noise came from somewhere far above her. She had no idea what could possibly make such a frightening sound. That is when she saw it.

There was a huge black blur diving right toward her. She had never seen a hawk before. She had only heard about them in scary stories that the young mice would tell to scare one another. The bird was approaching her so quickly; she had no idea what to do.

Missy let her natural instincts take over, at that moment. She ran for shelter. She began hurling herself through mud and over rocks, with the speed of lightning. The young mouse darted frantically around roots, sliding and tumbling to catch her footing.
The hawk dove for her, again and again. The bird was trying its best to catch the young mouse, stabbing the air around her. Suddenly, she found shelter behind a giant furry wall. Expect, that wall was moving.

The giant furry wall growled at the hawk; it was an earth-shattering sound. The little mouse had never heard a noise so big. Missy tensed up, prepared to run again when she heard the hawk screeching in retreat.

The giant brown wall was a bear; it moved its giant paw so that it could see the little mouse. She could feel the animal's gaze upon her. Missy was so fearful that she could hardly move; she had no idea what was to become of her.

"Hi, I am Paws. You're so small. I have never seen a creature like you. I like the heart on your fur," said the giant animal.

"I am Missy! Your voice is so loud and thundering. Thank you for scaring away the Hawk. I am not sure what I would have done without you," Missy replied, shaking.

"Those things are nothing but nuisances. I could keep you safe if you need protection," said Paws.

"I could never ask you to do that," she said.

"Nonsense, I could use a friend," he replied.

Paws took Missy back to his cave. The bear allowed the tiny mouse to burrow into his coat so that she could find refuge from the chilly rain. When she had dried off and calmed down, they got to know one another.

The bear was also young, though you'd never know it from looking at him. He was gigantic compared to the little mouse. He confessed to her that he was also an outcast. He had been left to make his way on his own. Paws lived in that cave, all alone.

Missy told her new friend all about her life back home. The way that she had always been isolated from the other mice because of the heart upon her chest. Paws liked the heart and suggested that the two could be friends.

It was then that Missy explained that she would have to go back home. She was only sent to the mountain to find high ground, as the valley below was flooding. She already adored Paws and wished that she could spend more time with him, but circumstances forbade.

"Bring your family here. You can stay in my cave! I can protect you all. When the rains have ended, I will return to the valley with you. I can live in the cavern near your field, and we can remain friends," said the young bear. Missy could have cried. This was to be the solution to all of her problems.

Missy met the owl days later, just as they had arranged. When the owl saw Paws, he almost flew away. Missy was sitting atop the bear's large head, waving to the bird.

The owl screeched in surprise before landing on a branch near the pair. They told the owl their plan. He shrieked again, but this time, with joy. Everyone back home had been losing hope, becoming more and more despondent. Now, if they could figure out a way to cross the field, they would all be saved.

The owl gave rides to the smaller animals. The larger creatures among the group found a way around the field. It was a longer walk, but they trekked on knowing that they would have a safe place to sleep. They all looked so majestic, walking along the mountain in a line, with a giant bear at the front of the charge.

When the danger had passed, and the rains were gone, the bear and the mouse became the best of friends. He was a vegetarian, so he got along with all of the forest and field animals quite well. Paws moved to the cave in the forest so that he could spend his days alongside his mouse friend.

Missy was celebrated as a hero for saving the mouse community and all the other woodland creatures. She didn't care much for the attention of her peers. The young mouse and the young bear marched together to the beat of their own drum.

Chapter 2: Dino Tales

Flip was a young pterodactyl. He and his parents lived on a ledge upon a high cliff overlooking the sea. His mother had fashioned a nest made of tree branches and other shoreline debris. Behind the cliff was a beautiful forest full of lush and tropical trees.

The young pterodactyl was green, with skin like that of a modern-day lizard. The tip of his mouth and his tail, both had patches of a brilliant red. He looked as though each end of his body had been dipped in lava. His skin covered wings were not yet strong enough to carry the pterodactyl in flight. Flip's head was still much larger than his tiny body, causing him to sling himself around a little as he walked.

Flip would climb up the remainder of the rocky cliff, above his nest, to meet his best friend on the shore just in front of the forest. A young brontosaurus named Pan had been the pterodactyl's closest companion for as long as either of them could remember. They went on adventures of all sorts together.

Brontosauruses grew to be massive. Pan was still young, but he was much larger than Flip.

To understand the construction of a brontosaurus, imagine a huge animal with the body of an elephant and the neck of a giraffe and the head of a gentle lizard. The creatures near the beach were a muddy shade of green, which better allowed them to blend into the forest.

Flip would waddle along beside his friend as they explored the lands around the shore. The young pterodactyl enjoyed making images in the sand, using his exceptionally pointed face as a drawing utensil. Pan liked surveying the local flora, which was as much about the sight of lovely flowers, as it was about the taste.

The pair would spend hours playing pretend and journeying through the trees. There was always an interesting (and sometimes dangerous) new creature to delight their senses. The forest was damp and filled with vines and brightly colored blooms.

A fog seemed to perpetually hang in the air around the friends on their trips through the forest. The air was perfumed by the exotic flowers around them. The atmosphere, when they were among the trees, was whimsical and mysterious. Flip was always nervous that something larger than them, and with sharper teeth, might break through the mist at any moment. Pan was never concerned by this; he was a dinosaur possessed by the spirit of adventure.

Flip's parents would expect him back at the nest, the moment the brilliant sun began to sink below the horizon. The young pterodactyl did not mind this rule, as he was not a fan of the night. He was always happy to be home, in the safety of his large nest.

The friends were walking along the forest floor just before dusk, one day. Flip had noticed that they were nearing familiar sounds. The thick fog, just ahead, prevented the friends from identifying the source of the noise. Pan seemed content to creep closer, which worried Flip because he wasn't sure he wanted to find the creatures responsible for the chirping.

The pair found a large tree to duck behind so that they could remain unseen. The sounds were coming from a small group of other pterodactyls, just ahead of the young friends. They sat amongst the canopy of the forest. Flip watched as the creatures hovered and then swooped through the air below them.

Pan and Flip had happened upon a group of younger pterodactyls, showing off their aerial tricks to one another. They all dove and rose again, to gracefully land on their respective tree branches. They were swift and intimidating in a way that Flip had never thought to associate with his own species.

The friends watched transfixed as the creatures above them, looped around branches. They elegantly swirled around the trunks and then ascended back to the canopy. Each of the pterodactyls would flap their wings for a few moments and then leave them extended, to glide through the air. They almost floated among the treetops.

Flip was instantly jealous of the creatures. He had been waiting so painfully long for the ability to fly. The group of young pterodactyls flew through the air with such purpose. His parents also took to the skies, but never in such a theatrical display. He wanted this ability for himself; it was his birthright.

Pan could not stop talking about the majestic way in which the pterodactyls swirled and zipped through the forest. Flip zoned out while his friend was praising the strangers, imagining himself in their place. He imagined flying alongside his long-necked friend. Pan always had to walk so slowly for Flip because he refused to be carried. He wanted to fly alongside his companion's stride. No more would anyone ever have to slow themselves down to allow Flip to catch up! He mused about the possibilities to himself. That night, the young pterodactyl decided to seek advice from his parents.

"Mom...dad? Why can't I fly yet?" The young pterodactyl questioned.

"Because some of our kind take longer than others. You will learn, dear," said his mother.

"Wait! So, I should already be flying? Why didn't you tell me?" Flip asked, frantically.

"Please, it would worry you. There is no need to worry. You will learn to fly, just like the rest of us did. It is only a matter of time. You must be patient," said his mother.

"Why am I so far behind?" He whined.

"It is natural, some pterodactyls just need more time," said his mother.

"Your head is huge. That is why. Physically, your wings can't support it yet. You will have to grow into it," added his father.

"Wow, Dad. Thanks for that," he said. Flip realized that his mother was just trying to explain the situation gracefully. His father had always been blunt. At least he understood after his dad's clarification. It made sense.

"Son, you will get there. Big heads run in the family. I have a huge head. My father had a huge head. You have a huge head. You will thank us for that huge head when you are out there trying to catch fish. It is a blessing; you just pay for it by waiting a little longer for flight," his father said.

"I am not going to wait any longer. I am going to teach my wings to work. I am going to fly," Flip replied.

"Son, I am afraid that it doesn't work like that," said his father.

Flip was determined to learn the hard way. The following day he set out to find Pan. The young pterodactyl was on a mission to beat nature. He was going to force his wings to carry the weight that they should be already bearing.

The small pterodactyl told his friend to stand completely still. He climbed from Pan's long tail to the tip of his head. Flip jabbed Pan in the back, with the tips of his wings as he worked to right himself. The pair were trying the experiment in the sand so that the short fall might not hurt as much if they failed. And they failed.

Flip picked himself up from the ground, dusting the sand from his small body. He was frustrated but not defeated. They were going to try until they saw results. After the tenth jump, the young pterodactyl swore to his friend that he had been able to flap his wings. Pan was not convinced that the flapping of one's wings meant anything, but he was happy that his friend was happy.

The pair tried again, over, and over. Flip was sure that he could train his wings to carry the weight of his head. He was sure that pure determination and will-power could help him in accomplishing this feat. He was able to flap his wings more and more. The pterodactyl then decided that it was time to take to the trees.

Flip waddled alongside his friend as they entered the forest. The pair trekked along until Flip found a tree that seemed suitable. Pan used his long neck to scoot some old leaves into a pile below the branch that the young pterodactyl intended to jump from. He tried his hardest to talk his small friend out of the questionable decision, but Flip could not be phased.

Pan aided the young pterodactyl in climbing, watching as his friend continued up the trunk on his own. He'd climbed much higher than any point Pan could reach, so he tried one last time to talk him out of the jump. Flip ignored his companion's words, and shakily maneuvered his way onto the suspended limb.

Flip took a deep breath and then promptly fell to the ground. The young pterodactyl screeched in pain. He had landed on his wing, causing a small sprain. Pan gently picked his friend up, placing him upon his back. He would have to take him to his parents so that they could heal his injury.

More than anything else, Flip's pride was wounded. He was so sure that he could fly from that tree branch. He had tried so hard, all day. Pan was amazed that his normally cautious friend had made such a careless decision. He felt guilty for having helped him.

Flip's parents sat opposite him in the nest, that evening. His mother had bandaged his hurt wing with palm leaves, and he was feeling much better. The young pterodactyl knew that he was about to receive a lecture. He could see the disapproval in their kind eyes.

"Why?" Asked his father.

"I was sure that I could do it, Dad. I had practiced all day! You guys taught me that hard work pays off, right? Well I worked hard," said Flip.

"We also told you that flying was beyond your physical capability at this time. Why didn't you learn that one?" His father replied, looking amused.

"I am sorry. I should not have disobeyed you. I really thought I could do it," Flip said.

"Look, Silly-o-saur, determination is great! It is how you accomplish things; that part is absolutely true. However, you can't just try something for a *day* and expect it to work," said his mother.

"And you can *determination* your way through a physical impossibility. That would be like me saying that if I practiced breathing fire really hard, for a day, that I could become a volcano. There are reasons why I can't be a volcano, son," said his father. "You can improve your skills! If you wanted to become a better sand-artist, that could be a thing you practice. You have control over that ability. It isn't part of your physiology; it is a choice you make."

"Then how do I learn to fly?" Asked the young pterodactyl, with frustration in his voice.

"Patience," his mother replied.

With those words, he waited. First, he waited for his wing to heal. It took weeks before the sprain was completely erased. Flip trotted about the beach, drawing in the sand to pass the time. Pan stayed by his side, watching the young pterodactyl as he worked.

Then he waited some more. Months had passed when Flip finally hit the growth spurt that he had been waiting for. His wings grew right alongside his body. He was no longer forced to waddle when he walked.

Finally, the moment he had been waiting for arrived. The young pterodactyl was walking to catch up with his friend when he noticed a glide-like quality to his stride. Flip attempted to flap his wings, watching in joy as they worked to lift him from the ground. The pair celebrated as he tried out his newfound flight.

It took Flip a while to master the skill in the way those pterodactyls from the forest had, but soon enough, he was living up to his name. He was soaring through the sky and above the canopy. He dove into the turbulent waters of the open ocean. The wind flowing all around his wings felt like freedom.

One day, Flip and Pan sat beneath a large tree in the forest. The pair looked up at the shiny orange fruit that hung from the topmost branches. Flip quickly flitted up to the top and knocked a few of them down, so that he and his friend could enjoy the new taste. Pan looked longingly at the canopy as Flip tore into his treat.

"My parents can reach those branches; did you know that? Their necks are so long. I can't wait until I am that tall," Pan lamented. Flip smiled at his best friend.

"You're going to need a little patience," he said.

Chapter 3: Dragon's Footprint

Helen was the daughter of one of the most respected knights in the land. Her father had been made into a folk hero before she was even born. The entire realm celebrated his heroic feats, including his slaying of a dangerous dragon. One that was supposedly a threat to the king and his castle.

Her father had been given titles and invited to court. He was nobility now, but he loved being known for his adventures and conquests. He now lived at the castle, while Helen and her mother stayed in their lavish countryside home. The women wanted for nothing and had servants to meet their every need. Helen had always known this lifestyle.

The young woman saw herself as delicate and dainty. She enjoyed art and singing, but she was not much for physical activity. Helen even avoided horseback riding whenever she had the chance to do so. Her one exception was the forest. She thought that it was beautiful and enchanted.

Helen loved to take long walks through the forest to clear her head. She would never do so for exercise, but it was a method of release for her. Sometimes she would lose herself in the haunting serenity of the stoic trees all around her. Quiet and monolithic, they appeared to the young woman, to be wise. Her favorite was a weeping willow that stood next to a hot spring.

The willow's branches gingerly traced the surface of the water. Helen thought the weeping willow didn't look sad at all; rather, she was elegant. She was being coy in the presence of the rest of the forest. Her sweeping limbs were always dancing in the wind.

Helen would return to her willow any time she could escape the house unnoticed. One day, she even became brave enough to slip into the hot spring. She had not planned for that moment. She took off her dress, leaving her long layered undergarments on, in case anyone was to venture by. The young woman leaned her back against the rocks that traced the outline of the water. The warmth of the liquid melted away every ounce of tension in her muscles.

The noble young woman allowed herself to sink further down. She laid her head back upon a stone and almost fell asleep. The warm breath of nature sung a lullaby to her soul, lulling her out of reality and gently toward slumber. She deeply inhaled, pulling the fresh forest air into her lungs.

She was shocked back into consciousness by a loud bang and then another. Helen felt a wave of panic running through her. She thought about ducking below the water's surface, but she was too curious to miss whatever was responsible for the noise. She grabbed a nearby stone and held it in her tightened fist, below the surface of the water.

The sound of men on horseback broke through the stillness again. The rhythmic clomp of their hooves against the forest floor was slowly becoming louder. Helen wondered for a moment if she should run. That is when she first caught sight of the magnificent creature.

There were giant winged beasts flying above her. The spring she had been relaxing in, caused a break in the canopy of the trees above her. She saw them soaring overhead. One circled to the back of the herd as if to protect the last creature in their formation. They were beautiful!

They were dragons. Suddenly, Helen's blood ran cold. She had only heard stories about these dangerous creatures. She had never seen one up-close. They were said to be evil, treacherous beasts. How could something so magnificent, be evil? Each of them was different colors, striking in their own way. The protective one was a deep sapphire tone; her scales were prismatic in the sunlight. Helen didn't know how she knew the dragon was female, but she knew.

They were being shot at. Arrows. The men on horseback were shooting at the flying beasts. The dragons were not retaliating; they were running. Helen could not yet see the men, but she could see their arrows and hear their horses.

Suddenly the blue dragon cried out. *Oh no! Had she been hit?* Helen worried. No, something was falling to the earth. A tiny beast had fallen from his mother, the blue dragon. He hit the ground with a horrible thud. Dust rose up around the creature, like a halo. He was the size of a baby if that infant were redistributed into the form of a dragon.

PLEASE

Helen could explain none of this, but she heard the mother's voice in her head saying one word. *Please*. There was no time for the young woman to think. She dashed from the hot spring, scooping up the small dragon in her arms.

He was beautiful. She knew that his name was Fyre; she was done trying to understand how. He had inky and prismatic scales, almost black with rainbows of light reflecting from his body. His tiny wings were the same deep blue as his mother's. Large black eyes blinked at Helen as she began to process the situation that she found herself in. The men were getting closer.

The young woman raced back to the hot spring, just as the men approached. She hid the small dragon beneath her unfolded dress and sat it to the side of her, as she pretended to relax in the pool. When the men came into sight with their bows drawn, she pretended to cover herself. She was still wearing her long undergarments, so the action didn't make much sense. The gesture seemed to work, though, as the men on the horses blushed and apologized. She bid them farewell, and they continued on their chase. It would have been much easier to hand the young dragon over, but the thought never crossed her mind.

When they were out of sight, Helen uncovered her tiny new friend. He was so beautiful that it made the noblewoman want to weep. She pulled herself from the water and cradled the confused young dragon in her arms. He was warm; she had not expected that. She always thought them to be as reptiles. She ran her thumb slowly over his tiny forehead. Helen could not stop her own tears; she was going to find his mother and return the poor infant to her.

The young woman knew that she could tell no one of what happened. Helen's own father could have been one of those men on horseback, many years ago. Her family was famous for hunting dragons. She would be alone on her quest.

Helen also anticipated that the journey was going to be difficult. She was frail; she never intentionally worked. Now she was going to be trekking through the forest, and she had no idea how long her task was going to take. She didn't even know if his mother had survived the men, but she suspected that she had.

The tiny dragon was completely quiet as she snuck back into her house. Helen found her largest bag and began to fill it with clothing and other things she thought she could use. On her way out, she took fruit and bread from the kitchen. No one was around to stop her or question her motivates, so she left without a word. Fyre was tucked beneath her arm. Helen saddled and mounted the fastest horse at her family's estate and rode off into the forest.

She innately knew which way to go, as if the mother dragon had made some sort of connection to the young woman. Helen stumbled along at first, struggling with her steering. She had avoided horses for most of her life, so she had only a basic understanding of how to make the animal go.

Soon though, she threw caution to the wind. She, her horse, and the tiny dragon were speeding along a path through the woodlands. Her mare was galloping with grace, over the rocks and roots on the trail. She wondered for a moment if the animals sensed the imperative nature of their mission.

Helen had never camped. The first night was difficult. She cuddled up next to Fyre, beside a tree. She covered herself and the adorable tiny dragon with layers of the extra clothing that she had packed. Her horse would occasionally stir, rousing her from a half-sleep.

The next morning, she heard hooves. The men, they must be in the area. That must also mean that she was getting closer to the mother. She mounted her horse and rode into the brush. Her vision was blurry from a lack of sleep the night before. Helen urged her horse forward. She could hear one of the men yelling. She had been spotted.

Helen cried out and held the small dragon close to her chest. He popped his head out of the swaddle she'd made from spare clothing. She had never been useful for anything in her life, she thought. The first time she found a purpose, she was going to be captured.

The young noblewoman could hear the men catching up to her. Their horses were galloping fiercely behind her. Helen's heart was pounding from her chest. Her horse was moving so quickly that she almost missed the markings in the mud, giant outlines of something.

Her horse slid down a muddy hill that neither of them had seen. She was barely able to jump off in time, as the horse tumbled and then stood again. Helen had used her own body to cushion the blow for the tiny dragon, who now clung to her chest. His wings covered his body, and he looked a bit like a little black heart superimposed over her own.

Helen pulled herself from the ground and stood before the men. They, and their horses, had managed the same hill with no trouble. The young woman was shaking as they drew their weapons upon her, displaced rage in their eyes. Why did they hate dragons so much? In her limited experience, the creatures were soulful and beautiful. They were to be celebrated, not feared.

The young woman turned so that her own back would be between the angry knights and the baby dragon. Tears rolled down her face as she looked up to see the beating wings of his mother. She appeared like a priceless gemstone floating from the heavens. Helen smiled; they would at least be reunited. No matter what happened.

Over the canopy appeared hundreds of dragons. They darkened the daylight above. Fire poured from their open mouths, though Helen knew that they would never use the flames within the forest. They were afraid of burning trees. The mother had passed this knowledge on as well, as though the connection were still formed between Helen and the dragon.

The knights looked on in dismay, dropping their weapons. A disembodied voice rang out through the trees, saying only "LEAVE." The men obeyed this ominous warning, mounting their horses and fleeing clumsily back up the hill. Helen cried at the sight before her; the beauty of the dragons was overwhelming.

She handed Fyre back to his mother. Helen marveled as her scales shimmered like deep ocean water, as the light reflected off of them. She rubbed the forehead of her favorite baby dragon, one last time.

This was the story of how Helen found purpose. The young woman spent the rest of her life fighting for the dragons. She helped build them habitats, she hid them when they were hunted, and she cared for the creatures when they needed her. Helen was enamored with Fyre, and when he was old enough, they worked together as a team.

People from villages all over the land would watch the inky dragon descending from the skies with a maiden riding upon his back. The friends would mingle with the locals, allowing the townspeople a chance to interact with a real dragon. No more poisonous folklore beasts. Helen became something of a celebrity herself. She molded her family's new legacy in the image of tolerance, all thanks to her giant wing-shaped black heart.

Chapter 4: Iridescent

Sam loathed magic. He hated it to his very core. His father had been lost to a witch's curse long ago. Sam did not care for any of it.

A young girl, in the village, had been going on and on about seeing a woman riding atop a dragon. Sam was sickened by the thought of a mortal endorsing that sort of frivolity, but there was no accounting for intelligence. The bitter young man told the girl to stop spreading that nonsense, before paying for his bread and returning home to his mother.

His mother wrapped her arms around her son, telling him not to look so dour. He sighed and tentatively agreed. Sam had become so cynical that he could not help but look upset.

He was always annoyed with something or someone.

Except for his mother. She was angelic, in his eyes. She worked as a medic in the village. There was so much compassion inside her that he almost felt guilty that he could not be more like her. They lived in a tiny shack on the edge of the village, with eight cats, because anytime the woman came across a stray, she had to save it. Sam thought that he had inherited nothing from her, other than her gray eyes. He loved her, still.

Their community had been thrust into turmoil. An area volcano had caused a forest fire, which had displaced other towns. Everyone was concerned that the flames would reach Section Three (which was the name of Sam's village). He thought that they were all concerned over nothing; they were not exceedingly close to the disaster.

From beyond the gaps in the logs that made up their house, Sam could hear villagers outside speaking frantically. His mother noticed the commotion too. She quickly threw on a cloak and rushed outdoors to see what everyone was concerned about.

They were in need of medics, two townships over from Section Three. Sam stood in the threshold of his shack, listening in horror as his mother agreed to go help. She would leave the same night, after insisting that he stay to protect the house (shack) from bandits.

"What are they going to steal from us? We are peasants. Are they going to take cats? Because please," Sam said. His mother smiled sweetly at the young man and embraced him again before leaving. He already knew there was nothing he could say to stop her.

It only took two days before Sam was bored out of his mind without his mother. He quickly realized that he spent most of his time talking to her. She really was a saint. The young man paced across the floor of the shack for hours before deciding that he would take a walk in the field behind the village. It was a lovely spring evening; there was nothing stopping him from going to greet mother nature.

Sam quickly made his way through the village, and then past it. There was a vast open field, lined by forest on two sides. The castle took a side, and his village took a side. The rest was untamed woodland. The young man didn't venture beyond the tree line because he knew magic lived beyond those borders.

The young man was enjoying a long stroll beneath the setting sun. The air was perfumed with the scent of lavender and roses. He breathed in the soft spring air. Even someone as grumpy as Sam could find reasons to be happy outside in nature.

There was a rustling from the trees to the young man's side. At first, he resisted the urge to investigate. If there was something in the forest, he wanted no part of it. Sam reluctantly continued to meander through the field.

The young man's curiosity finally got the better of him. The low rustling continued, and he was slowly becoming convinced that he was being watched. Sam could not think of anyone who would want to stalk him from the forest, but paranoia and fear are not rational emotions.

He crept closer to the edge of the field, where the tree line met the grass. The young man could feel his heartbeat beginning to accelerate. From the brush leaped a small rabbit, who then dashed across the open field. The animal was propelling itself with impressive force. Sam breathed a sigh of relief until he turned his eyes to the forest.

There, in front of him, a horse-like creature rested upon a bed of dead leaves. The animal was as white as the driven snow, with a long and prismatic mane. Atop its majestic head, a pearlescent horn.

The horn was not a straight or perfect cone. It was twisted around itself, creating the most elegant spiral impression. Sam had never seen anything like this before. He was so preoccupied with the intensity of the scene before him, that he had not stopped to think about *why* there might be a unicorn resting at the edge of the forest. He carefully approached the scene.

As he advanced toward the creature, it gazed directly through his eyes and into his soul. The experience was jarring; he could feel its reluctance. The unicorn wanted Sam to leave, immediately. There was no question in his mind that it wanted to be left alone. He could relate to the being's distrust, but it only made him more curious.

The young man held his hands out in front of him, so the creature would see that he was not going to hurt it. Sam slowly walked toward the unicorn. The horse-like thing in front of him began to tense, as though it might try to stand and flee.

He spoke to the creature in the same voice that his mother would use with injured or frightened people. Sam had watched her work, calming villagers who'd only moments before, been hysterical. Her patients always ended up surrendering to her gentle nature, a nature Sam was sure he did not possess.

The unicorn relaxed and let the young man approach. There was wisdom behind the creature's gaze. Its eyes were the color of a summer storm. Even though it was injured, the creature seemed to radiate with stoic energy.

It was injured. Sam noticed that the unicorn's leg appeared to be burned. It must have come from the forest fires. There was a sudden aching in his heart for the pain that the creature must have experienced. He tried to reconcile this inconvenient empathy with the fact that he hated magic.

There was never really any debate. Sam's mother had given the young man more than he ever realized. No matter how angry or cynical he became, he had her heart. Mercy and love dominated his mother's entire being; her son could only pretend that he was different.

Sam knelt beside the creature to assess the damage done to its leg. The burn was not profoundly serious, but he knew that the unicorn was probably in pain. It likely hurt to walk such a long way on a limb that had been licked by flame.

The young man carefully moved his hand to the creature's mane. He cautiously reassured the unicorn of his intentions by touching its neck. The animal just continued to gaze at him, as it had from the moment it had laid eyes on him. Sam briefly wondered if the magic made unicorns more intelligent than horses, or if this was just a very pretty horse with a horn.

"I will return to you, please don't worry," said the young man. The unicorn seemed to nod slightly, almost instinctually. Sam could not tell if the creature had understood his words, but it was responding to his voice. He could not help but feel like he'd just spoken to a person who tried to pretend they didn't hear right after accidentally making eye contact. *I am insane for putting this much thought into analyzing a head nod.*

Sam ran home to grab a mixture of herbs that his mother had concocted specifically for burns. He also threw adhesive and bandages into a sack. He looked around for anything else, with his eyes finally landing on the fruit that he had bought at the market earlier that morning; every day, he would purchase a few pieces from town as part of his routine. He raced back to his new patient in the forest, returning to find the creature exactly where he had left it.

Sam bandaged the unicorn, who reluctantly allowed the young man to address its wounds. The entire time he worked, he could feel the creature's intense gaze upon him. It was nervous about the young man's presence; he knew the tension in its stare.

Upon tending to the creature's injuries, Sam handed the unicorn an apple. It gazed at him silently, almost as though it were annoyed by the gesture. Its stormy eyes gawked at the offending fruit.

"Not because you are a horse. I just thought you might be hungry. I don't know what unicorns eat," Sam said, laughing a little. To his amazement, the unicorn seemed to accept this explanation. The creature took the apple from his hand, allowing itself to enjoy the sweetness. "I know that you probably can't speak, but I would like to know your name if you have one. I am not sure if there is any way that you could tell me. I may be stupid for asking..."

"Gust," said the unicorn. The words sounded inside Sam's head. He could tell that they had not been spoken. The creature was somehow speaking directly to him. He was taken aback by the experience.

Sam did not want to like the creature. He'd distrusted magic so much, since his father's passing. He could not help but feel a connection between himself and the hurt unicorn. He could tell that Gust was not intensely pleased with the prospect of liking Sam, either.

He asked the unicorn if it needed help standing, which Gust seemed to decline. That night, he brought the creature a blanket. Sam sat next to his injured friend, eventually falling asleep beside him. The young man wanted to make sure that no one with worse intentions stumbled across the vulnerable unicorn, healing in the forest.

In the following weeks, Sam stayed beside Gust. At first, he told himself it was only to guard the creature. After a while, it was evident that there was an affinity between them. The unicorn enjoyed Sam's company and vis versa.

Gust and Sam slowly became friends. Sam learned that Gust had lost members of his own family to mortals. The creature had his own biases, something that they both overcame for their friendship.

The unicorn stayed right outside the village until eventually, Sam and his mother were able to move into the forest. They'd saved enough money to build a house, no more shack. When Sam introduced his mother to the unicorn, she gasped. She slowly approached the creature, petting his iridescent mane. Of course, Gust loved the woman immediately.

Sam's mother cared for the unicorn as if he were a son. Sam treated Gust as though he were a brother. The pair would go on adventures together, each living out their lives happily in the presence of the other.

The young man who thought that he might never feel compassion for anyone other than his mother was given a heart that day in the forest. He needed a friend more than he needed anything else. Sam mended the unicorn's leg, and they both healed.

Chapter 5: Wolfpack

The wolves of the Gray Stone Mountains were quick and effective hunters. Other animals refused to cross the creatures. They roamed the countryside in a pack, sparking fear in the hearts of all those that they encountered.

The whole pack resembled the world that they called home. They were a smokey color with black noses. Flecks of white shimmered in their coats, like freshly fallen snow. The animals looked both fierce and beautiful. They mirrored the mountains they roamed.

They claimed a vast territory, patrolling all the way from the fields in the valley below the mountains, to the snowcapped peaks in the highest altitude. The wolves were fearless and enduring. Long winters threatened other species, but this particular family of canines was clever. Again and again, they slid safely away from situations that should have spelled their downfall.

Every other animal on the mountain, and in the valley below, respected the wolfpack. The bears would pass silently by, allowing the wolves to go about their business with no hindrance. Other predators also avoided causing trouble with the creatures.

Lower down on the food chain; life was not so breezy. Rabbits scampered through the night, trying to find their next home. Deer froze in the forests below the mountains, to listen for footsteps of any variety—a small community of foxes that darted about, looking for their next meal.

The brilliant auburn fur of the foxes set them apart from the rest of their environment. They were the color of fallen leaves in autumn or a smoldering flame. Hunters would come from far and wide to find for the chance to find one of these striking creatures. Their fur was unique to the area, long and graceful.

The tips of their tails looked to have been dipped in dark ink. Where others of their species had white fur, the Gray Stone Mountain foxes had dark brown or black accenting the crimson. The creatures were so sought after that they had to learn to adapt. The animals had become masters at stealth and hiding. They allowed no weakness within their ranks.

One fateful day, a mother fox gave birth. None of the other animals noticed that anything was strange with the kit. It would not be until the tiny creature began to grow that the skulk (or group of foxes) would notice there was an issue.

Infant foxes are born with dark fur. They are smoky gray, and black. Their fur turns its customary crimson shade as they begin to mature. When Eva was born, she entered the world looking precisely as she was supposed to.

Pups and kits that were born around the same time as Eva were slowly getting their color. Their dark fur was blushing slowly as they began to turn the majestic autumn shade that they were meant to be. The young fox was beginning to worry that something was wrong with her, as her fur was staying dark. In fact, the areas around her ears, nose, and tail were downright black.

Eva's parents tried to pretend as though nothing were wrong. They encouraged their daughter to continue interacting with the other young foxes as though she were as red as anyone else. Their skulk valued uniformity so much that they were beginning to worry for

Eva. She could be cast out if she were found to be too different.

The young fox did not help her cause by being completely different. Eva blended into her surroundings almost perfectly; she was, by default, very stealthy and quick. It was slowly becoming apparent to all the other foxes, that she was less interested in hiding and more interested in adventure. Adventure was not something that the skulk approved of. There was no room for bravery in their world.

The foxes valued the ability to run and hide. They needed to be especially quiet and exceptionally good at blending in. Eva was curious and impulsive. She wanted to explore the world around her; there could be none of that, especially when she was already abnormal.

Eva loved the open fields and the forests. She loved venturing into the mountains and watching all the animals that called the area home. Rabbits fascinated the young kit, and she loved to watch them leap around. She was even known to chase a bunny or two, just for fun.

The sound of the rushing river that cut through the woodland, excited Eva. She spent so much of her time watching the bears catch fish from the stream. The animals did not seem to mind her presence, which was unusual. They allowed her to sit and observe for hours.

She'd discovered their acceptance of her presence after being spotted one day. One of the massive creatures happened to venture up behind her as she was watching the river from behind a bush. The bear had stopped to gaze at the young fox for a moment deciding, no doubt, if it were going to eat her.

Her heart was pounding, but she did not flinch; she was ready to fight if that is what the bear wanted. Eva believed he saw the ferociousness in her eyes, allowing her to pass his test. Whatever the reason, the massive animal let her continue her observation. Following the incident, the young fox was open about her presence at the river. She bravely sat upon a boulder with her elegant black tail curled around her body.

While she was missing, on one of her adventures, her skulk made a difficult decision. They held the meeting in a clearing, in the center of the woodlands. There was news that wolves were nearby, so the foxes were already on high alert. Eva's parents were in attendance, but they dared not speak. The foxes were all so nervous by nature that her family had seen this day coming for a long time.

Eva had reached maturity. She was technically capable of surviving on her own, the skulk believed. They exiled her from the community. She was to leave immediately. They argued that her impulsive and adventurous nature was going to place them all at risk.

The young fox did not take the news well. She mourned the loss of her skulk and her parents, the way any rational being would. Eva cried alone in the forest for a week, only stopping to eat and sleep. She felt betrayed. She was perhaps the stealthiest fox in the whole group; they just could not handle that she was different in any way.

Weeks passed before she tried to return to any sort of routine. The young gray fox sat upon her familiar boulder by the side of the rushing river. The sound the water made as it clashed with the rocks was soothing to her troubled soul. She mindlessly gazed out over the rapids, cursing her need for exploration. The bears were batting at salmon as they jumped upstream.

"Ash, one of yours, watches us as we fish. She is a curious little thing. We have grown to miss her when she is not around; she is our good luck charm!" Said one of the huge brown bears. Eva felt her heart sink; she knew they were referencing her. *Who do they think I am?*

"One of mine?" Said a throaty feminine voice from behind a tree on the other side of the roaring river. "How did you even know I was here!?"

"I know the moment someone steps paw around these parts. And I am referring to your pup, the one that sits on the boulder. She is here now!" Said the bear. Eva got the feeling that she should run, but she was too interested in what was happening.

A magnificent gray wolf peaked her head from behind the tree. Her long cloudy fur was slightly ruffled, as though she'd been running through the forest. The creature was so elegant. She was also one of the most feared throughout the whole area. The bear had only let Eva watch because he thought that she was a wolf pup. *Oh no.*

"That isn't mine. I am not even sure that that is a wolf. We are the only wolves around here. What an interesting creature," said Ash.

"Not a wolf?! She looks exactly like you," said the bear. He directed his attention to the young fox. "What are you?"

"I am a fox," Eva said. She was so frightened at that moment, but she refused to show it. She could not let the two predators in front of her know that she was terrified. "I am just a discolored lone fox. I am not looking for trouble; I just like watching your fish."

"The nerve! I should have eaten you months ago!" The bear exclaimed.

"Stop! I claim her. Don't hurt her," said Ash. "I wasn't going to hurt her. I've grown attached. I just said that I *should* have eaten her months ago. I definitely would have if I had known she was a fox," said the bear.

"Young fox, you are safe. Maybe you should return to your pack now. This is not your side of the forest, and you might get hurt," said the wolf.

"I come here almost every day, and I don't have a skulk...er... pack, anymore," Eva replied.

"What? Why not? Were they hurt? What is your name, young fox?" Asked Ash. The fox and the wolf were yelling back and forth to one another across the roaring river. Eva watched in awe as the majestic smoky wolf jumped her way across the water. She maneuvered to the fox's side, using stones and boulders as landing pads. Eva was amazed by the wolf's grace.

She had never seen one in the flesh. She gawked as the beautiful gray beast sat down beside her, on her boulder. The moment did not feel real to Eva. Ash was incredible, elegant, and frightening. Eva selfishly wished for a moment that fox from her old skulk would pass by and witness the pair sitting side-by-side.

"My name is Eva. My skulk abandoned me because I was not red and because I am not boring and afraid all the time," the young fox said, with a little sass in her voice.

"You have no family?"

"Not anymore. I am learning to be happy on my own, though," said the fox.

"That shade of red is a crime against nature, anyway. Where do they camouflage? In fire? You need a family, young thing. I have so much family. I would like to share with you. It's wonderful that you happen to look like us already, but just know that we have never kicked a wolf out for looking different. We would never kick a wolf out for being interesting. We are far more likely to adopt foxes than we are to ever kick a member of our pack, out," said Ash. "You are clearly meant to be a wolf-fox, anyway."

Eva was so touched by Ash's words that she could not speak. She'd felt as though her family was wrong for denying her, but the fact that they'd all agreed that she was bad, made her feel crazy. The young fox wholeheartedly decided to join the wolf pack.

Ash became a mother to the young Eva; Eva became the eternal pup. The descriptor fit because she was so bouncy and full of energy. The young fox was the first to volunteer for exploration missions. She flourished under the guidance of the wolves, who encouraged her adventurous nature. They protected her brave heart.

The gray fox was loved by the pack as one of their own. Eva expected that they would treat her like an outsider, but the stares never came. She was immediately a family member. She slept curled up next to them, ate with them, played with them, celebrated with them, and mourned with them. The wolves were her family, and she felt as though she belonged with them, in a way that she never had with her own skulk. Eva had never known unconditional love until she joined their ranks.

A day of reckoning arrived, with no notice. She was out hunting with her pack when they came across a bright red fox. The wolves chased the animal, all the way back to the skulk. The same skulk that had ousted Eva. When the young fox realized what was happening, she stood between the terrified foxes and her own wolf pack. She told her new family that they must spare the foxes.

The wolf pack agreed, with no hesitation. Suddenly, the frightening hunters became playful puppies as the sneers faded from their faces. The foxes were still horrified, but they were also amazed. They watched, shocked, as the kit that they had rejected saved their lives. Eva's own parents watched her leave with her fierce new family, a family who had just listened to and respected her wishes. A family who saw the young fox as one of their own.

Chapter 6: The Mermaid and the Shark

Pearlville was a vast underwater kingdom. The merpeople that populated the deep ocean city had never been seen by mortal eyes. Some had glanced passing sailors and pirates, but they kept away from human lands. It was forbidden to interact with land creatures because they were known to be dangerous.

The brave gulls that ventured among the mortals told tales of their exploits. The mermen would gasp in shock at the way the humans interacted with one another. The merpeople were peaceful, so they stayed away from such horrors.

The underwater castle was made completely of unused and old seashells, lending to its brilliant color. The houses were accented with pearls that had been gifted to the creatures, from the oysters that lived among them. The mermaids lived harmoniously alongside the fish that called the deep sea their home.

Dew was a particularly lovely mermaid. She and her father lived within Pearlville, in an unassuming blue shell-house. She could peak out of her window and see the castle, which sat just down a small slope. They were poor, in mermaid terms, but Dew adored her life.

The mermaid's tail was a brilliant iridescent lavender that complimented her deep chestnut skin tone. Her black hair flowed in tight coils around her waist. She had the face of a doll with large hazel eyes. Dew was also known for her grace; she swam as though she were a part of the ocean current. The young woman's father wanted to use her natural beauty to push her into gaining a place within the castle. He hoped that if he dragged her to enough parties, that she would be invited to court. He knew that if a member of the royal family saw his daughter, they would realize that she belonged among the nobility.

The young mermaid had other interests. She could not have cared less about the ambitions of her father of finding a place in the castle. Dew was obsessed with finding and cataloging new species of fish. She loved hearing the stories that the new creatures told.

Every time Dew came across a new fish, she would feel a rush of excitement. She was invested in protecting ocean wildlife. She gathered experiences from each creature, feeling as though she were journeying to the ends of the earth, herself. Each day, she would venture further and further from Pearlville limits, in search of new faces.

There were limits for a reason. There was only one thing that the merpeople feared more than mortals. Sharks roamed the waters near the city, often drifting through as they traveled toward new coasts.

Dew had been taught that the creatures were deadly. She had never seen a shark with her own eyes, but the descriptions gave her nightmares. They were supposedly giant gray beasts with fangs as long as men. Their eyes glowed red in the deep ocean, as the evil within the beast struggled to shine through.

Everyone knew someone who knew someone who had seen a shark. Dew had trouble tracking down reliable first-hand experiences, which frightened the young mermaid even more. She knew enough of the beasts to know that she did not want to find herself near one of them. Dew had gone through entire classes in school dedicated to shark avoidance.

All of that cumbersome information seemed to melt from her mind, as she explored the area outside of the city. Dew felt as though she was being watched, but there was no one around her. She continued to swim along the ocean floor.

The young mermaid was greeted with the most amazing sight. She passed the normal hills and valleys that she normally explored, pushing just a little further. Dew found herself swimming above a massive drop-off. There was a cliff below her that looked to extend hundreds of feet down into utter darkness.

She was close enough to the surface of the sea, that light still touched her. Sunlight bathed all of Pearlville. Dew had never seen a section of the ocean that light did not touch. She was frightened and fascinated.

Dew knew that she should absolutely not go down there. Just looking over the edge made her nauseous. She was too nervous to even swim over the giant pit of blackness. She should definitely not go down. *Right?*

The young mermaid lingered on the edge of the shelf, contemplating her next move. What should she do? Her gut told her to leave the situation alone. Maybe she could return with someone who knew more about this sort of thing. Who was she kidding? She was the only one who cared about pits in the ocean. *Imagine the fish down there!*

"Don't do it. There is too much pressure down there," said a voice from behind her. Dew froze. It must have been the creature that was watching her only moments before. She slowly turned around.

Her blood ran cold. Just off to her side, hiding behind a small hill in the sand, a shark. Probably a shark, anyway. The thing was so strange looking. It was reasonably large and gray, but its head seemed to veer off in two different directions. It was a little goofy looking.

"What...what on earth are you?" She said, cautiously approaching the creature.

"I am a hammerhead," the thing said. He had an eye on either end of his protruding face-sides. Fascinating. She touched his T-shaped head; he felt like a whale or a dolphin.

"Oh, thank goodness. I thought you might be a shark. I was going to dive headfirst into that abyss," she said, only half-joking.

"Listen..." he said.

"No! You're a shark, aren't you!?" She demanded.

"Yes, I'm a shark. I am not going to hurt you, though. I just find mermaids to be so interesting. I thought maybe we could talk," he said.

"Of course, you would say that. And of course, you would try to convince me not to venture into the pit. You want me to stay right here so you can eat me. I am not going to fall for this trap," Dew said.

"Wait!" She heard him cry out as she began her descent down the cliff. Less and less light was reflecting off of her iridescent tail as it propelled her into the darkness. It felt as though she were swimming forever. She was surrounded by black.

Then there was a tiny glowing light. She gazed at it in amazement. Dew had never seen anything like this either. Lots of firsts on that day.

The brilliant neon glow penetrated only a small halo around the orb. It was just a bulb in the inky blackness. Dew swam cautiously toward the light. She stopped just in front of it. The mermaid was just able to make out a stem-like attachment that seemed to be suspending the ball.

Gnarly teeth suddenly appeared as a mouth opened in front of her. Dew shrieked and backed away, but the thing chased her. It was not nearly large enough to be a serious concern, but she did not want to be bitten by the abomination. She swam lower into the void.

There was a bioluminescent jellyfish just ahead of her. Dew thought that she might be imagining things, she watched as its body pulsed with the movement of the water. The glow was magical somehow, and hazy. Or her vision was hazy. She did not feel all that great.

The last thing the mermaid remembered seeing was that jellyfish dancing in the deep dark. It was ethereal. The creature looked like a phantom, floating along into the abyss.

The mermaid awoke as she was being pulled along. Her head hurt, and she was more concerned with the ache than she was with the fact that her arm was wrapped around something strange. Dew allowed herself to drift back to sleep. A few moments later, she was snapped back to reality; she was zooming through the darkness. She had no idea which direction she was being taken.

There was another light ahead. It was not sunlight, but it was also not a fish. The illumination was bright enough that she could make out the form of the hammerhead. Her arm was draped over one half of his face. That was probably the only way he could lift her without biting, she thought.

They were drawing closer and closer to the weird new lights. There was one to the left and one to the right of a large transparent bubble, that was also lit up on the inside. Dew could vaguely make out two stubby arm-like appendages on either side of the bubble.

The shark must have been interested too because they were venturing so near to this weird transparent bubble. Dew, who was only just able to hold her head up, gasped. Inside the bubble sat a mortal woman in a chair. The lady's jaw also hung open in shock at what she saw.

The woman slowly stood up and got as close as she could to the glass that protected her from the sea. Dew took her arm from around the shark, who had stopped swimming toward the contraption. She approached the bubble. She had never seen a mortal before. They looked so much like her, except for the legs.

The mortal woman placed her palm against the glass. The mermaid returned the gesture, with both women smiling at one another— their touch as only separated by the transparent material.

The shark nudged the mermaid, who bid a sad farewell to the mortal. Since she was awake, she held onto her new friend's back as he propelled the pair toward the surface. He swam much faster when she was not attached to his face.

"Thank you for saving me. I completely misjudged sharks," said the mermaid, as she sat in the sand atop the cliff.

"You were wrong about some sharks. Always be wary, though. Had you ever seen a mortal before?" He asked.

"No, never. You?" She replied.

"No. I never expected to meet my first down here," he said.

"You should probably also be wary of them," Dew said, laughing.

The pair spoke for hours about their respective homes. Dew wanted to hear all of his stories. The hammerhead was chatty and had plenty of tales to tell. She was utterly fascinated by the creature, as she had never seen anything shaped like the shark in front of her.

Dew told her father about her encounter. At first, he was angry that she had disobeyed the rules and swam past city limits, but then he was curious. She took him to meet the hammerhead. The shark introduced himself as Joe. Her father was dumbfounded; he had never met a creature like Joe.

Dew's father arranged a meeting with the royal court so that he might introduce them all to Joe. The merpeople were thrilled; Joe was a hit with everyone. He was told that he could enter and leave the city as he pleased, so long as he maintained his gentle nature.

Dew and Joe became good friends. The mermaid borrowed him when she needed to travel outside of Pearlville city limits. The pair ventured all around, exploring the reefs and meeting the brilliantly colored creatures that call them home. They joked with one another that one day they might even return to the abyss.

The young mermaid was no longer afraid of the darkness. She had essentially faced two of her largest fears in one single day, coming out of the equation with a new best friend. It would be much more satisfying to come across that horrible orb fish again, with a hammerhead shark lurking just behind her.

Chapter 7: The Curse

There once was a man named Nicholas, who lived in a small village nestled in the mountains. Resources were limited, so; families were packed into their small houses. Nicholas (or Nick) lived with his grown children and their own children. He enjoyed the chance to spend extra time with his loved ones, even when space was tight. The old man especially cherished hugs from his daughter Erin. Her embrace would bring light to even his darkest days.

Nick had a problem, though. The man worried more than anyone else in the entire mountain range. Every day, he looked to the sky as if it might fall down on top of him. There was no small detail that Nick did not agonize over, endlessly.

He had, surprisingly, raised very calm children. The rest of the household spent a good deal of time trying to calm Nick down. He would return from grocery trips to the village with shaking arms and long-winded warnings that found their life in the gossip that the townspeople told.

"There is a cougar lurking around outside! We must stay in for the rest of the week!" Nicolas shouted as he sat sack of vegetables upon the small wooden table.

"Where on earth did you hear that?" Asked his only daughter, Erin.

"Old Miss Derin said she saw a mountain lion stalking through her backyard last night!"

"Nonsense, she probably saw a cat. You know how she is about being overdramatic and blowing things out of proportion," said Erin. "Well, the woman swears it was a panther. I, for one, believe her," said Nick.

And so, went most of the old man's interactions. Nick would go to town, become terrified, and then return home. Sometimes, he would just imagine up a completely nonsensical threat and then spend the rest of the night lecturing his family about their immediate danger.

Nicolas had no idea what this paranoia would soon be his undoing. The man was walking back from a routine visit to the village. The journey involved making a sizeable trek through the forest, which already made the old man uneasy.

He walked along in silence; his ears were sharply tuned to the world around him. On that particular day, the wind was blowing through the rustling leaves with some force. Nick's head would jolt from one direction to the next, in an effort to locate where some *thud* or another had originated.

Nick began to notice the way the shadows were moving across the forest floor. He listened as leaves seemed to crunch in every direction. His heart began to beat faster as his mind raced through all the scary possibilities. *Could it be a lion?*

The old man began to pick up his pace. He found himself walking faster and faster. It seemed as though, the quicker he moved, the more fearful he became. It was as though the terror was feeding on his reaction to the world around him.

Finally, the anxiety came to a boil. Nick dropped the bags that he had just acquired in the village and began to sprint. All he wanted was to arrive home in one piece. He was now convinced that he was being followed. There was nothing he could do to escape the invisible enemy.

Nick was so intently looking over his shoulder that he did not see the village witch walking just ahead. She was carrying a heavy load of logs back to her shack, hidden deep within the forest. The witch was moving slowly, carefully. She had already lost a log or two and decided to keep moving because of the effort that the transportation was taking. She was a small and thin elderly woman with sharp features and intense blue eyes.

Nick collided with the witch, as he was sprinting. He knocked all the wood from her arms. He looked at the mess that he had made and helped the witch from the ground, by extending his arm to her. She gladly accepted. He apologized as he ran away.

The witch was a witch, but she was by no means uncivilized. She would have forgiven Nick right that moment if he had stayed to help her gather all those heavy logs again. He had messed up her morning and then just left her stranded to deal with the consequences, and for what? He was being chased by nothing.

The witch quietly mumbled a spell beneath her breath as she struggled to gain control over the rouge logs. The old woman spat her words disdainfully, supporting herself as she bent to pick up the wood, with one of her arms bent and her hand resting upon her lower back. Nick needed to learn manners. She was just the person to teach that old man a new trick or two.

That night, while the family was sleeping, Nick heard someone calling his name from outside. It was a young and feminine voice. The witch used it so that he would not feel threatened. Nick still felt threatened. The old man crept up to the door, with a large board poised behind his back. He was ready to swing it at a villain at a moment's notice.

The old man slowly opened his front door, as the child's voice continued to call for him. Nick was not going to take any chances. He was ready to defend himself from whatever child army awaited him in the darkness outside.

Nick peered out into the inky night. He saw nothing. He took a few more steps away from the safety of his house, moving with a slow caution. Then he saw her. The witch stepped from the edge of the tree line with a lit candle in her hands, the last element of her curse. He had to watch her blow out the flame, and then her spell would be complete.

Nick stared helplessly as the witch puckered her lips and extinguished the light. The old man felt his body begin to change. He was growing a thick coat of fur and sinking to the ground. Suddenly, he had taken the shape of an animal. The man opened his mouth to question the witch, but all that came out was "*Bahhh*."

He was a goat. The man yelled and yelled, with each call being expressed as a *bah*. The witch had disappeared from the edge of his yard.

Nick was more frightened than he had ever been.

The coming weeks were difficult for both Nick and his family. His loved one grieved him, believing that he had been taken in the night or had simply left. Erin lit a candle for her father every single night, leaving it by the door. She wanted to ensure that he could always see if he chose to return home to them in the dark.

Nick had to witness their sadness, which made him despondent too. He was forced to watch as his family believed that he had just forgotten them. It shook him to his core.

Slowly though, he transitioned to the new normal. Nick learned to eat grass. The family had simply accepted the goat's presence in their yard. Erin sometimes even looked at the animal as though she thought it might be her father.

The old man decided that he would use his newfound horns to guard the family home. He would sleep during the day and keep watch during the night. This was the last vestige of his old life that he clung to. Something was happening inside him though; something he could not explain.

Goats are not tasked with all of the same responsibilities as mortals. They are free to live out their days in freedom and relaxation. Even the old man was forced to enjoy the calm, as he marched along the mountainside at dusk.

There was a floral perfume to the air, something he had not noticed in so many years. The wind was gentle, like the touch of a loved one. Lush trees shook from the breeze beneath a sherbet twilight sky. Even the old goat was enamored with the beauty of nature.

Slowly, his fear began to melt away from him. Nicholas began to cherish his days in the sun. He slept at night again, watching the stars shift overhead as he drifted into dreamland.

He skipped to greet his family as they entered and exited the house. They all loved the old goat. Erin, especially, would devote hours a day to the animal. She would even read to him, sometimes.

One night, Nick was sleeping on a bed of leaves. He was dreaming of fields of lollipops beneath a hazy summer sun. Clouds of cotton candy formed shapes like animals above the goat's head. He was suddenly jolted from his rest by noise from a nearby bush.

There was a rustling in the foliage, something loud enough to wake the old goat. He stood up and began to advance. When all that unnecessary fear had left Nick, he had become something else entirely. He was brave.

Before him, stood a mountain lion. The goat stomped a hoof into the ground, preparing himself to charge. He was not going to let this oversized cat harm a single hair on his family's heads. There was a tension between the two animals.

Nick knew that if he ran away from this fight, he would probably not be able to return to the yard. The mountain lion would have claimed the territory for itself. The creature would then be able to attack any member of his large family as they left the safety of the house. He would never let this happen. The old goat huffed.

The mountain lion hesitated at the sight of the goat's face. The animal could tell that the goat fully intended to engage in whatever conflict arose from the confrontation. There was a glimmer in his eye; he was unafraid of the big cat.

She backed off slowly, retreating back into the forest from which she came. The goat did a triumphant dance in the yard. He spun around and around, kicking the air.

Nick did not yet know that all witch's spells were conditional. As he celebrated his victory, his body began to change again. His spine straightened, and he shed his fur. The old man was becoming a human again.

He could not believe his eyes. The old man wept tears of joy at the sight of his arms and legs. He knew exactly what his first matter of business would be, right after a good night's sleep in his own bed. Nick opened the door to his house, only able to see from the light of the candle that Erin had left burning.

The following morning, he was awoken by a scream. A happy scream. His daughter stood at the foot of the old man's bed, looking on in disbelief. He sat up and outstretched his arms so that he could embrace her; he had waited all night.

Nick was determined to never let himself fall back into the habit of dwelling within his fear. Being a goat had changed his entire mentality. The old man was going to devote himself to enjoying his time. He would still meet challenges as they arose, but he would not seek them out.

The witch had seen his irrational terror that day. She decided that she would make an act of bravery the condition that broke the curse. When the elderly man had threatened to fight the mountain lion, her spell had been challenged, and the curse fell apart.

The old witch smiled to herself as she watched the old man walking back to the village the next day. She realized that he must have finally overcome his most enduring flaw. Nick was afraid of nothing, except for maybe that tiny old woman with the sharp features and the intense blue eyes.

Chapter 8: Rainbows

A unicorn had come to Alice in her dreams. No one in her village had ever seen one in person; magic was rare in her area. The creature was striking—one of the most beautiful things that she had ever seen.

The unicorn had a pearlescent rosy horn and pastel coat the color of lavender. The creature's mane was the same pale pink of her horn. Flecks of iridescence reflected rainbow light from streaks in her mane.

The unicorn's name was Rose. Like all magical creatures, Rose had powers. Her abilities allowed her to conjure mud and clay from the earth and form it into shapes. She used this talent to sculpt. Rose could also paint and sing. The most interesting of all of the unicorn's gifts was her ability to create visual art.

Alice first learned about these powers when she met the creature in a dream. The young lady was feeling drained. Her week had been dragging by. Every day, she only felt more and more exhausted and bored. Her days were gray.

She had been having a difficult time sleeping. Alice would toss and turn in bed at night, with no way to calm her thoughts. She was becoming more agitated, in general, as time went on. The young woman had no way to express herself. She was creatively blocked up.

That night, when she finally drifted off, Rose was there. The unicorn was not apparent at first, but it was as though she was placed upon a path to meeting the creature. A meeting that fate had already ordained a long time ago.

Alice watched her frilly blue nightgown ruffling in the air as she floated to the ground. The world around her was illuminated by a soft lavender glow, as though dusk were casting her shadow over the land. The young woman was placed down in the middle of an enchanted forest.

The trees were swaying back and forth in the gentle wind. They were dancing slowly, to a melody that radiated from the heart of the woodland, something haunting, nostalgic, and beautiful. The voice that Alice heard singing was so very similar to that of her mother when she was a child.

The voice seemed to warp and wind through the woods. Every tree moved in time with the rhythm. Birds chirped along to the tune, adding a strange percussion to the notes when needed—the young woman hummed along with the forest.

The air smelled of honey and roses. Alice walked along a path in the forest floor, her bare feet making contact with the ground as she moved. She felt safe, warm, and comfortable in this world. The world that she had imagined in her dreams.

By chance, the young woman looked to the skies above. The beautiful pink clouds above her head were swirling. There was something so comforting in the slow way they spun around one another. The sun was a glowing neon orb or orange as it was setting beyond, sinking below the hilly horizon.

A creature that looked to be a furry ball with large innocent eyes approached the young woman. It held out a tiny paw to her. This creature was the most adorable thing that Alice had ever seen.

"Who are you?" She asked the furball, as it led her along a path through the enchanted forest.

"I am a thing that you have created in your dream world. I am here to help you," it said, in a high-pitched squeak.

"No! What? Are you saying that I made all of this? And you?"

"I am saying exactly that. I am going to lead you to someone who is not a figment of your imagination, though. If you will follow me please," it said.

Alice followed the thing down the long trail. There were so many interesting things that they were just zooming by with no notice. A singular dancing rose grew from the brown leafy brush. It called out to the pair as they passed.

"There. Just ahead!" The thing said, pointing to a clearing in front of it.

That is when Alice met Rose for the first time. She looked radiant, by the light of lavender dusk. Her coat reflected a striking pale pink. She was the most beautiful thing that Alice had ever laid eyes upon.

"You are most certainly not real," Alice said to the unicorn.

"I am. I am speaking to you through your dreams because I am not with you. I can't venture into your land. We are meant to be friends, but you will have to find me," said the unicorn.

"Why are we meant to be friends?" Asked Alice, immediately regretting the question for its bluntness.

"I have almost the same information you have, so I can't really answer that for you. All I know is that I can speak to you in your dreams. You also already know where I am, but you are going to have to search inside yourself for the answer," Rose said, stomping a beautiful hoof into the ground. There was luminescent dust floating in the air around the two new friends. "I have to commend you;

your dreams are stunning." Rose watched the glowing particles swirling around them.

"Only my dreams. My real life is gray and boring," said Alice, reaching her hand out to disturb the matter in the air.

"You are starving your imagination. Maybe that's why we are connected? We are both creative," said the unicorn.

"You got that from me saying that my life was boring?" Asked Alice, accidentally blunt again.

"No, look around you. The world inside your mind is bursting with creative intent. You are probably only so bored because you have not focused on your abilities. You should paint, sculpt, sing or write. You must find a way to feed your imagination before you lose it. I bet that when you have done this, you will find me," said Rose.

Alice was suddenly jolted awake. She felt crazy for everything that she had just dreamed of. She also felt as though she wanted to grab a pencil and a sketchbook. The young woman began rummaging around her room until she found what she was looking for.

The young lady took the unicorn's advice in the coming weeks. She began to produce sketch after sketch. She would paint the images that she liked the most. Alice began painting her dream world. She loved the colors in the reality that she had made up. The unicorn was the most beautiful thing she had ever imagined.

As she kept drawing, her skill began to advance. Soon, she was crafting many elaborate scenes with such exacting detail.

Alice would have never guessed that she was capable of such a skill. The unicorn had called her a friend. Alice would spend her hours daydreaming that the unicorn from her dreams was real.

Alice stopped feeling so gloomy; she did not even notice the change at first. There was something beginning to stir inside her. A whole world was slowly coming to life. Every night she would dream and then wake to draw the scenes from her slumber.

Eventually, she needed to seek out something more challenging. She would go and observe nature with her sketchbook in hand. She would draw the scenes before her in a fantastic way, adding elements of fairytales. She loved drawing the adorable creatures that she had met in her first dream.

Every now and then, the unicorn would return to her while she slept. The pair began spending time getting to know one another. They were becoming friends inside the confines of her slumber. She would treasure those memories when she woke up.

Alice took to painting more real-life scenes. She especially painted one mountain over and over again. It had a very distinct shape, like a horizontal lightning bolt. It was jagged and wild against the backdrop of a dark sky.

The young woman became obsessed with this mountain scene. She thought more than once that maybe her unicorn friend was there. Alice had no way to find some random mountain in a sea of geography, though.

The seasons were changing slowly. Alice continued meeting her friend in her head. Rose told Alice all about her own fantastic life.

She had seen so very many interesting things in her short time.

The young woman had bonded with the unicorn more than she ever had with any mortal. They were the closest friends. She could feel that they had been fated to meet and that all of existence was waiting for them to come together. Finally, Alice caught a break.

Her father returned from the market one day, recounting the local gossip. There was a snowstorm bound for the Caspin Mountains. The word sounded like magic to Alice. It stuck in her mind immediately. She could not forget Capsin Mountains.

The young woman immediately fetched a carriage for the mountains. She was hoping with all that was inside her; the ridgeline was jagged and irregular. *What if the landscape*

from my dreams is just how mountains look?
What will I do then?

They were not. She knew the moment that she first glanced at the landscape; this was where she was meant to be. Alice ordered the carriage to progress down a slender and dangerous twisting road. She watched as the gray rock, and surrounding forests began to show a light dusting of snow.

The flakes floated from the heavens like they were being controlled through magic. Alice had always loved the way snow looked, especially when it had just fallen. The carriage driver seemed ill-at-ease. They continued along the mountain trails until she saw the scene that she had been looking for.

Directly in front of her was the vista that she had always seen in her dream. It was surreal to look at the same mountains in person. The moment seemed so much large than her, and she shook with excitement. A rainbow stretched across the sky above her, landing somewhere in the forest to her side.

She stopped her carriage and grabbed her drawings from a sack beside her. The young Alice ran into some woods before the driver could stop her. She ran as quickly as she could into the trees. Alice was determined to find out if the unicorn was real. She knew that if she could find the end of that rainbow, the answer would be there.

Her questions were answered soon enough, as she happened across the scene. The unicorn stood before her, in a clearing, at the end of the rainbow. Rose had a look upon her face as though she had been waiting for her friend. She cried out at the sight of her.

Rose brought something to life inside Alice; she had started that first time that the young lady had dreamt of her. They were fated to be friends; their destinies were intertwined. The pink unicorn woke up Alice's imagination. They would go on to find out that Alice did the same for Rose. The pair were inseparable. Even though she was tangible, Rose was always going to be the dream at the end of the rainbow.

Chapter 9: Roar

Art was a young t-rex who lived deep within a Jurassic jungle. His parents were some of the most feared dinosaurs in all of the land. Even the ground seemed to tremble beneath their massive feet as they walked along.

Art was different from the rest of his family. He was not fearsome or mean. He did not want to intimidate the other dinosaurs; if anything, he wanted to befriend them. The young t-rex watched helplessly as his parents always accidentally ran every other creature away. They were so intimidating.

Both his mother and his father were gigantic. They had gray skin with sparse feathers. Their teeth were the intimidating feature. Huge fangs hung from their mouths, which looked like muscular traps that were ready to snap shut at a moment's notice. They looked truly deadly, and no one was ever going to get to know any other side of them.

None of the other dinosaurs were ever going to know that his mother loved to dance. She would sway beneath a full moon, to the sounds of crickets and other forest insects. His father was goofy; no one would ever know that either. The young t-rex listened intently to the horrible jokes that his father told, saving each and everyone for the day that he might have a child of his own.

Art could not help but feel lonely, deep in the heart of that jungle. Something was missing from inside him. He wanted friends. The young t-rex would have given anything to have some friends of his own.

All of the other young dinosaurs were forbidden from speaking to Art, as his parents were so very intimidating. He dreamed of having a friendship, even just one. The t-rex thought of his loneliness almost constantly.

One night, when he could not stand to be alone with his thoughts any longer, he ventured out into the forest alone. He was going to take a walk to clear his mind. A good hike beneath the shimmering starry sky was more than enough to ease his troubled mind, he hoped.

He did not have a destination in mind. Art walked and walked. He continued on until he no longer recognized his surroundings. The young t-rex had never been to this part of the jungle. There were so many new sounds, all demanding his attention at once. The cool night air was inviting his imagination to dream of the most fantastic beasts.

That is when he came upon them. There was a small community of mixed herbivores in a clearing to his right. They were all still awake and stalking amongst the trees; there were a few large dinosaurs mixed in; they had large bodies and long necks.

The smaller dinosaurs ranged in shape and size. There were some with spines on their heads and others with boney crowns. They each walked around slowly, picking the leaves from the various trees in their vicinity.

There was something so peaceful about the way they seemed to exist among each other. They were all quietly chatting as they went about finding their meal. There were so many different creatures, all living together in a community. Art was immediately jealous of the animals in front of him; he had never known such brotherhood.

A small green dinosaur approached him. Even though Art was young, he was still twice the size of this creature. It stepped closer to the baby t-rex with caution.

"Hello, my name is Leaf. Who are you?" It said, in a soft and timid tone.

"I am Art. Just a...you know. Traveling herbivore, looking for friends!" He said. He was sheltered beneath the shadow of some trees, so he was not quite visible to the other creature, from the light of the glowing moon.

"I see! We could be friends. Would you like to come to find food with me?" Asked Leaf. The small dinosaur's eyes were on the sides of his head. The t-rex was amused by the way he had to turn his entire face, just to look in Art's direction.

"Yes, I would love that!" He said, not realizing what he was signing himself up for.

The pair ventured off into the jungle in search of fresh leaves. The smaller dinosaur seemed to have a tree preference. Art had never tried to eat anything green. He imagined that foliage would just taste wrong. He was right.

The t-rex struggled to chew through the leaves. He tried not to show the disgust upon his face. He was happy to choke down vegetation if it meant that he had a new friend. The pair chatted and got to know one another. Art lied about being a t-rex but was honest about his struggles with loneliness. He knew that if he told Leaf the truth about his species, that he would never want to see the baby dinosaur again.

From that night on, the friends met in the same place and went looking for leaves to eat. Art got better at hiding his disdain for the taste. Sometimes he would chew the brush with his teeth and then spit it out when Leaf was no longer looking. He had no idea how all those herbivores managed this lifestyle.

Their bond grew more and more. Art was also growing. The young dinosaur did his best to hunch over in the company of his short friend. Leaf had once asked Art why his teeth were so sharp, to which Art replied that his species ate a lot of tough fruit.

Art's family were scavengers, but they looked like predators. He would return every night to his lonely pocket of the forest, free of whatever small dinosaurs his parents had accidentally terrorized during the day. Art loved his family, but he wanted more than a solitary existence. He wanted friends.

Leaf invited the young dinosaur into his own tribe. The older creatures looked at him with suspicion until he pretended to eat some flowers in front of them. He met and laughed with the dinosaur community every single night, and those interactions filled his heart with joy. Then he would sneak back into his own section of the jungle.

One night, he arrived in the clearing where he always met Leaf. There was no one to be found. It seemed as if the whole community just vanished. His heart sank. He would not know what to do if something had happened to all of his friends. He heard a rustling from behind a bush, turning to see his friend hiding inside it.

"What are you doing in there? Where is everyone?" Art asked. The leaves of the bush were shaking as though his friend was frightened.

"I stayed behind to warn you. We are being hunted by a group of raptors and allosaurs. I did not want you to be eaten, but now we are both stranded out here. They could be anywhere," Leaf said, frantically.

"Is everyone else, alright?" The young t-rex asked.

"Yes, for now. They are all in hiding in some cave. If the raptors find them, though, they won't have anywhere to run!"

"Why on Pangea did they pick a cave?" Art asked.

"Being out in the open is too scary for any of us, right now," said Leaf. Art felt his heart sink. His friend cared so much for his safety that he risked his own life to ensure that Art wasn't ambushed. He could have cried out.

"Don't worry Leaf. None of them around going to bother us. I can promise you that we are going to be alright," said Art. A strange sound erupted from all around the dinosaur friends. It was the low rumbling of laughter from every side. The baby t-rex moved in front of his herbivore friend. "Don't worry."

"Art, we are done. They are all around us. I have really enjoyed getting to know you, thanks for always coming around," said Leaf. That was such a heartbreaking thing to hear. His friend had resigned to his fate, using what he believed to be his final words, to say goodbye.

The vicious-looking raptors finally emerged from behind their respective trees. They all looked so slender and sinister. Beady little eyes shone out as they surrounded the friends. Art wondered if that is what he looked like to other dinosaurs, or if maybe he would look that way someday. The thought saddened him.

Art took in a deep breath and roared as loud as he could. It was a formidable sound, even from one so young. The raptors looked surprised for a moment, before laughing with one another again. They began to creep closer. The young t-rex called out again, using as much air as he possibly could.

"Nice roar, kid. It isn't going to help you or your friend," spat one of the raptors.

Then Art heard what he was hoping for. There was a distant thudding; it shook the ground. Consecutively, the sounds rang out through the night.

"I thought you said the t-rexes lived on the other side, Sly!? That sounds like a t-rex to me," one of the raptors said to another.

Art's father slid into the clearing with a terrifying look upon his face. His fangs caught the light of the moon, offering the raptors a glimpse into their potential future. He roared into the night, shaking the trees around them. The raptors fell on top of one another as they rushed to escape.

The adult t-rex looked at his son with confusion. Thank goodness they had heard his roar; it woke them from a dead sleep. Art's father had rushed through the forest, leaving a gap in the brush, in his wake.

"I am sorry dad. My friend was in danger, and his whole family is still in danger," Art said. His friend gawked at the behemoth before him. He was still frightened. "And I am sorry Leaf; I should have told you the truth a long time ago. I am not a herbivore. I am just a young t-rex." Leaf was still looking at the monster of a dinosaur standing before him.

"You're making friends with herbivores? Not that I'm judging, but that is a little strange for a t-rex," said his father.

"I just got so tired of being lonely. You guys accidentally scare everyone else away. And if I can only be friends with dinosaurs like raptors, then what is the point? They are awful. You should meet his community! They all live among one another in harmony," said Art. "Leaf, please know that we don't kill. My family is made of scavengers."

"I forgive you, but this is going to take some getting used to," Leaf said, at long last.

"I have a funny idea. Let us guard your community for a while. As he said, we don't hunt. It is too much trouble with our disproportionate arms," Art's father waved his small limbs in front of himself to demonstrate their size. "Take us to meet your community elders, and we can discuss a plan. Maybe we can just exist among you."

"You can trust us," said Art. Leaf agreed, knowing that his friend would never hurt him. The community of herbivores was shocked but also deeply thankful to have a protector. The raptors must have been watching them already because they never showed their faces again. Art's parents moved their home to the community, and they would stand watch over the group of gentle dinosaurs. Art and Leaf remained the best of friends.

Chapter 10: The Whole Barn

Suzy was an intelligent cow. She'd had the free time to learn about all sorts of things that her parents were unable to. She knew about bugs and their many potential functions. She watched flowers bloom beneath the summer sun. The young brown cow even took notice of the passage of time, creating her own sundial system with an overturned pail and a branch that she'd found.

More than anything, she loved to observe. She loved to watch the way the world came together to allow for the competition of tasks. Suzy took great pride in whatever project she had decided to devote herself to.

Suzy's life was strange for a barnyard animal. Many farms expected much more of their livestock; she had heard some disconcerting stories. Farmer Rick was not most farmers, though. He was a kind and peaceful old man that maintained his farm mainly for the company of the animals within.

He sold his crops and the eggs produced by his hens, but mostly he worked to ensure that all of his animals were taken care of. This allowed them all the free time to find their own interests. Many of the other cows spent their days in the field, gossiping amongst one another. The pigs enjoyed dirt and not much else. Horses and mules spent their hours running back and forth over the lush green pastures behind the barn.

Each of Farmer Rick's many animals lived a life of luxury. There wasn't much else than any of them could ask for. Wide-open pastures beneath clear blue skies; the air was fresh and therapeutic. Babbling brooks peppered the forest behind the property, and the animals were often visited by deer. Suzy had never known anything else, and she was deeply thankful for her luck.

One day, Farmer Rick called all of his animals into the barn. Suzy propped herself up against a stack of delicious hay, to listen to his speech. She assumed that he would tell everyone that there would be a new addition to the herd or that they needed to conserve resources. She was unprepared for the words of her guardian.

"Listen, I haven't said anything because I did not want to worry anyone, but there is something, I am going to have to tell you. We are losing the farm. A freeze last weekcompletely destroyed the strawberry crop, and now the bank is threatening to seize the property if I can't produce the money. I didn't want to tell you guys, but I also felt that it would be unfair to spring it on you when the farm goes to market," said the farmer.

There was a stunned silence throughout the barn. None of the animals could believe what they were hearing. There was a sense of dread that hung heavy in the air that day. Hopelessness dampened the mood of every creature.

The farmer also looked forlorn. He had worked so hard to care for these creatures, and there was no way to ensure that someone else would do the same. He could not stand to lose his family's property in this way. He was beside himself with guilt and fear.

"We are going to figure something out. I will not let anything happen to any of you, I promise," he said after a long pause. There is no way that I am going down without a fight."

It was in those moments that the animals were all given a purpose. They must somehow find a way to save the farm so that they could continue to live the life that they all loved. They wanted to support the man they all loved, their guardian. There was no other farmer like Rick; they have all won the lottery when they'd found their place among his herd.

The animals met that same night to brainstorm ways to help the farmer. The pigs volunteered that they could donate some of their dirt to the townspeople, but no one else was on board with their idea. The hens said that they would ramp up their egg production. This was the only idea that every animal could agree on.

The following weeks, the hens did nothing but lay eggs. They produced one after another. All of the other animals were on hand to bring them anything they might need to make the process easier. Some even gave up half of their meal, so that the hens could eat more.

The plan seemed to be working alright. The farmer was thrilled when he came to check their eggs every day. He took the excess away and immediately drove to the market. He knew that his animals were helping him. He could feel it in his bones.

One quiet evening, men with suits came to knock upon the door to the farmer's house. They handed him a white envelope that appeared to be from the bank. He opened it to find that he still had an astronomical balance left upon his bill. Rick was going to have to come up with some more ways to make money fast, or else he might have lost everything.

Farmer Rick's house was beautiful and old. The floorboards creaked as he walked along with them, but it reminded him of all the years those walls had witnessed. So much life had been played out behind the windows. His own childhood replayed in his memory again and again. The farmer brainstormed, pacing back and forth across his bedroom floor.

He called all of the animals to the barn again. He looked slightly more optimistic than last time, but Suzy noticed that worry still tugged at the corners of his eyes. Farmer Rick spoke slowly and methodically.

"I know that you have been producing more eggs. Unfortunately, our bill is quite high. I was hoping that I might have your help with another plan," he said. All of the animals vocalized so that he would know they were in agreement. "I remember my father running out of money once when I was young. He had a similarly close relationship with his animals. Together, they put on a festival in the pasture. He raised more than enough money to pull us back out of debt, but he owed far less. I am not sure that this will work, but with your help, we can try."

That was all the small brown cow needed to hear. She immediately set to work, figuring out what each animal could do for a festival. The hens could produce eggs. The grownup cows could make milk. The rest of the animals could perform in some way. For this to work, she knew that they all had to get started immediately.

Suzy devoted the next two weeks to learning tricks. She taught herself to jump over the potbellies. She learned to balance a pail atop her snout. Suzy even helps coordinate the performances of other animals.

Farmer Rick went to town and bought all sorts of lights and game booths. Suzy worried because she knew that all of those things costed money. She did not like the idea of him having to spend more, in case their plan did not work for some reason.

Fliers had been hung up all over the town, and people were excitedly buzzing about Farmer Rick's fair. There was even going to be a singing contest and a chilly making competition. Everyone in their small rural area was excited to see what the farmer was going to do.

A lady neighbor named Maggie came over the night before. She and Farmer Rick spent all evening and night, baking cakes and cookies.

They made all sorts of treats so that they might have prizes to give away.

The horses, donkeys, and cows all worked to clean the pasture the night before. The horses were eager to give rides to the village people, as none of them had ever even worn a saddle before. The pigs were eager to lay in their mud.

The day of the fair finally rolled around. The turn out was incredible. There were so many people arriving to see Rick's farm and his amazing performing animals. The barn had been converted into a game room that was being monitored by one of the horses.

Someone was playing the fiddle in the pasture so that the donkeys could dance. Each of the creatures stood upon their hind legs and formed a line. Their front hooves were resting upon the creature in front of them.

Deer from the local forest had arrived, volunteering themselves to children. Suzy was surprised at the sheer number of people who were interested in petting the deer. They made quite a splash with their contribution.

The cows were all doing different things. Suzy performed her act to a small crowd as they gawked at her abilities. She was a smart cow and found it easy to keep everyone engaged with her tricks.

The gossiping cows now mooed in harmony. They had made the most interesting song with their various voices. They had also produced milk for the occasion, but their talented singing was earning them all quite the crowd.

Farmer Rick brought Suzy a plate of the winning chilly. The young cow leaped around in appreciation. She looked at the man who had been taking care of them all; she was so grateful for him. She was in awe of the steps he was willing to take in order to ensure that his farm was cared for.

There was a sudden gasp from the crowd, followed by cheering. They were surrounding the dirt pits just beside the barn. Even Suzy found herself surprised by the commotion. She and Farmer Rick hurried over to the scene.

The farmer could not believe his eyes. He watched as one of his pigs drug a hoof through the mud. They were drawing. They were creating mud portraits of the fair crowd. They were being paid handsomely for doing so. The money was piling up in a pail that they had stolen from Suzy's sundial; she could not help but laugh. She had no idea that the pigs were talented in any way. She had especially not expected them to be creative. Their whole personality seemed to revolve around the amount of time they could spend in their mud.

When the crowds finally dissipated, the farmer began to count the money. He and Maggie took all of the cash into the house so that they could add it up and see how much more they needed to save the farm. The two of them were in the house for an eternity before he called all of the animals to the barn again.

The farmer had a piece of paper with some figures penciled upon it. He looked sad. His mouth was downturned, and he was silent for a while before addressing the crowd of animals.

"I have some good news and some bad news. The bad news is, that the pigs made five times as much as everyone else... but the good news is that we get to keep the farm! And then some!" The farmer shouted, smiling. He almost had Suzy; she was ready to run away from his words.

Cheers erupted from all over the barn. The pigs were especially vocal. The young brown cow decided that she was going to have to ask them to teach her how to draw.

Suzy's heart was full. The entire barn had come together to solve their problem. She wasn't sure that any of them would be able to come up with a winning idea, but she was wrong. The animals around her were her family. Even the ones that never left the mud.

Chapter 11: The Silver Scale

There were so many different types of dragons. Some could spit fire, ice, or water, and others could manipulate matter. There were dragons that could grow things with their mind. There were others who could become invisible. The one common denominator that united all of these beasts was their ability to run, jump, and fly.

Dragons were spectacular athletes. They treasured their physical abilities above everything else, except for maybe bravery. The magical creatures would be the first to rush into danger and also the showiest about their efforts.

There was nothing that any of the creatures loved more than flying. It was an impressive feat, on its own, but the dragons would always make a spectacle of their adventures. Each year, there was a competition where dragons from all over the realm gathered.

The event was similar to a triathlon, except that the focus was upon flying and traversing tough terrain. Those who won this race were celebrated as heroes. Every single young dragon longed to compete and win The Silver Scale.

Much like the name implied, the winner was given a silver scale in place of one of their own. There was a specific metallically gifted dragon in charge of the trophy. One could walk among the dragons and spot the past winners from the way their chromium scale shimmered in the sunlight.

Ret was a small dragon with ambitions of winning the prize. His smaller size meant that he was quite a bit faster than the larger and heftier of his kind. The creature had dreamed of the victory lap from the moment his father told him of the race.

Ret was a lava colored creature, with ashy accepts all over his body. Large black spines arose from his back. The dragon had a uniquely sharp-featured face, which lent to his superior aerodynamics. He was built for the competition.

The young dragon trained for hours every single day. He was determined that his practice should pay-off on race day. Ret knew that dragons from all over the realm would be in amongst the competitors, which made him all the more fierce about his routines.

Ret lived in a rainforest beneath an active volcano. He used the landscape to his advantage when it came to exercise. The young dragon would fly around and around the open crater at the top of the mountain.

He would watch in wonder as it spat fire and magma high into the air. Against his father's advice, he used this intensity for his own training. He would fly through the raining magma, dodging the embers and the liquid heat. Ret practiced until he was sure that he was the quickest dragon in all of the land.

His smaller stature also allowed the dragon to fly for longer. When others would tire out during tedious journeys, Ret was always energetic and eager to continue. He had been naturally given so many advantages, and the creature when the extra mile to ensure that none of those gifts went to waste.

On the day of the race, twenty other dragons lined up along the starting line. There had been qualifying regional competitions beforehand to determine the most deserving candidates. Ret had sailed through all of those races too.

The young dragon looked at all of the creatures lined up beside him, and for a moment, he felt doubt. There were so many massive and intimidating beasts that all wanted the same thing that he wanted; how could he have a chance? Then he remembered, to spite their imposing stature, he was the most able to fly quickly.

Ret looked at his claws for a moment, before the beginning of the race was signaled via a shrill dragon that stood off to the side of the action. Ret's father watched nervously as his son took to the air, already securing a lead. He was so small and quick, but his father could not help but worry.

The scene was picturesque. The neon orange sun was slowly melting into the horizon. It seemed as though they were flying straight into the flame, which brought Ret even more comfort. It felt like home.

The first leg of their journey was to take place over a grassland. Ret soared, doing the occasional flip just to show off his skill. He was already ahead of the other creatures. The young dragon smiled as he felt the summer wind beneath his wings.

To his surprise, so many of the dragons then began to catch up. He supposed that maybe it took more to get the larger competitors up to his speed. But once they were, there was no stopping them. Ret began to feel anxious about their ability to catch up to him.

The young dragon was neck and neck with another beast for a while. They seemed to switch places every few minutes. The competing creature was completely blue, like the darkest depths of the ocean. His scales sparkled in the waning sunlight.

Ret could not help but appreciate the effort that it must have taken for a larger dragon to meet his speed. He felt a moment of closeness to the other competitors. They all trained for and desired the same thing. They had all prized The Silver Scale above everything else in their lives for years.

The race continued as the dragons whizzed past one another. There was a constant struggle along the front line, to see who might keep the lead. Ret was pretty certain that he could maintain his speed for much longer than any of his larger counterparts. He knew that they must be beginning to feel the fatigue of strenuous activity. When the other creatures slowed, it would be Ret's moment to shine.

The next leg of the race was going to be above the raging sea. The competitors were coming up on the shoreline. Ret watched as the waves crashed in around themselves below him. He and the blue dragon were still trading places, back and forth.

It was not long before the sun had gone down completely, and all of the participants were flying over the open ocean. There were vast stretches of water in every direction. The sea could be intimidating at night. Ret worried for any of the dragons who began to tire over the waves.

He was secretly keeping an eye on the blue dragon to his right. He listened for the beating of his counterpart's wings, to verify that he was still in the sky. Ret had always been compassionate in that way. It was a trait that the young dragon had inherited from his father.

Ret's dad was not interested in these sorts of competitions, but he respected his son's ambitions. The older creature was concerned with the well-being of his community and his family. He often volunteered to guard the rainforest against those who might seek to sneak in and steal the timber, which would destroy their home.

Ret found himself daydreaming about his father when he was suddenly shocked back into reality. The young dragon realized that he had not heard the beating of the blue dragon's wings in some time. A jolt of panic ran through him. Could the other dragon have just found a faster route? They were all going to the same place; it made no sense that he was no longer in the front with Ret.

The small lava dragon thought the situation over, intensely. He had been working for years for this race, but he could not let another dragon suffer. His only hesitation was that the blue dragon had simply fallen behind, losing speed.

Ret decided that he could not risk the other dragon being hurt. He swerved around and began his way back through the night. He had only moved his attention for a few moments, but the blue dragon could be anywhere. He could see nothing at the surface of the sea; it was too dark.

Ret, waited for a group of dragons to catch up. He flew alongside them, asking if they had seen the blue dragon. None of them had. He then asked if any of them could use light or breathe fire.

A green dragon peeled away from the herd to join him. Ret was so relieved. He knew there was no way he could help anyone on his own. He heard a strange beating of wings behind him. He turned to see all of the dragons from that small group, following him.

Ret could have cried. They were all willing to give up something that they had worked tirelessly for. He thought that he would be the only one, but in an instant, they were all behind him to support the search. He wanted nothing more than to find his blue counterpart before anything bad happened on the angry open sea.

The green dragon began to breathe fire toward the surface of the moving water. At first, there was only stillness. They flew back and forth for a while before a creature from the group suggested that they give up. They were too far behind to catch up now, but the others were worried that they might also become tired.

Ret could not let them give up on the talented blue dragon. That was when they noticed a disturbance on the surface of the water. Something large was swimming below them, but some distance away. Ret's heart began to beat faster.

They found the blue dragon doing everything that he could to keep his head above the water.

The collective managed to pull him from the ocean's grasp and fly to a nearby island. The creatures all rested the night, watching the full moon hanging high above them all.

"You were going to win. If you had not turned around, then you would have won. Why did you save me?" Asked the blue dragon. Ret sat with his tail wrapped around him, on the sandy beach. The pair were watching the waves come in.

"There is no way that I could have left you. You are so talented. I relate to you so much, and we have never even met. I would never leave you in the ocean to fend for yourself," said Ret.

"I have no idea how to thank you. They will give you no prize, and you will have to compete again. I just can't even explain it to you... I thought that I was done for. I thought that even if you would have noticed that I was gone, that you might not have turned back," said the blue dragon, as he wept. The salty wind dried his tears as they fell.

"Well, you are safe now. If I am being honest, I could not have saved you alone. I would probably have sunk right alongside you. I was not expecting any of the other competitors to help me search for you. I was scared too," said Ret.

"I can't believe that the community came together at that moment. I would never have believed it if I had not seen it. I owe you my life. My name is Aqua, by the way," said the blue dragon.

"Well, that's ironic. You do not owe me your life. I could honestly always use another friend, though, if that is something that you would be open to?" Suggested Ret.

"I could always use a friend too," said Aqua.

The small group of rescuing dragons returned to the starting line the next day. There had been a lot of worry over their return. They had missed the end of the race, by hours. Ret's father had already been organizing search parties to locate his son. He wept with tears of joy upon the sight of them all flying in.

None of them won, but they all made a sacrifice that turned them into better creatures. The story of their venture was told far and wide. The following day, it was decided that they would each receive a diamond scale. The small group of dragons would be the first to ever be fitted for such a precious gem.

Aqua and Ret went on to become best friends. The pair competed in the race again the following year. Ret won and was finally able to claim his own silver scale. It meant surprisingly little to him after the previous year. Ret and Aqua left the race, their diamond scales sparkling in the midday sun as they flew away.

Chapter 12: Stripes

Sandy was a tiger cub who lived with her family in the jungle. She had always been vivacious and playful. The young tiger looked up to her mother, who was also strong-willed and independent.

Her mother was a beautiful, brilliant orange with thick dark stripes. Sandy could think of nothing more majestic than her mother's coat or her striking amber eyes. The cub was just a walking miniature of her mom, which was a source of great pride for her. She could not wait to be as intimidating, strong, and elegant.

The cub spent most of her days alongside her mom. She watched her climb trees, and the pair played games that were meant to teach agility and speed. The young tiger had never much thought of the world outside of herself; there was no need. Everything a cub could have wanted lay right at the tip of her paws.

The jungle was lush and green; it was also surprisingly quiet when the cub and her mom were around. Sandy enjoyed climbing the twisting trees, jumping from branch to branch. She took pleasure in the way the forest smelled after the rains.

Sandy was deeply protective of her relationship with her mother, but tigers were made to be solitary animals. As she grew, it became more and more imperative that she learn to venture out on her own. The cub resisted making those trips into the jungle; she enjoyed the company of her mom.

Slowly, the transition was becoming inevitable. She was going to have to learn to take care of herself. Sandy's mother knew that she could not protect her cub forever. She was going to have to allow the young tiger to blossom in the way that she was meant to.

Sandy's mother sat in front of her. The tiger's massive paws rested in the jungle dirt. The cub marveled at the way the colors of her mother's coat seemed to melt into one another; the orange transitioned to side around the sides of her face and along her chest and stomach. There was no other beauty quite like this, Sandy thought.

"You are going to take a trip into the deeper part of the jungle today. It is time. You will return home to me right after, but I want you to venture into the trees and observe the forest," said the large tiger.

"Well, I would rather not go without you. I am not ready!" Said Sandy, pacing in front of her mother.

"You will never be ready until you do it. One of the most fundamental parts of being a tiger is showing bravery. You must always rise to meet your challenges," said her mother.

"What is the point? What could be out there that I have not already seen?"

"So much! There are so many animals that hide the moment they see me. Have you ever noticed that you don't hear so much as a bird's chirp on our adventures through the trees?" Asked her mother.

"What is a bird?"

"Exactly! This way, you must go and explore alone. You know that I am only a roar away, should anything happen. You will walk along the same path that we always use. You will be safe because the other animals already know who you are," said the large tiger. Her eyes looked like deep pools of honey when the light reflected upon them.

"How do they know if we have never met?" Asked the cub.

"We are scary to the other animals. They see us coming (especially when you are with me), and they hide. I doubt that they will all hide from you alone. So, you will go," said her mother.

Sandy reluctantly agreed that she would take a walk through the forest. She was not interested in meeting any other animals, because none could be so brilliant as her mom. The cub only wanted her mother's approval. That was her goal in following along with the time-honored tiger traditions.

Later that day, Sandy awoke from a nap. She shook the dirt from her coat and stretched her small legs. The cub was intentionally slow with her actions, as she knew that she was inching closer and closer to the hour of her walk.

The small tiger told her mother that she was ready, reluctantly. She approached the path they always took, cautiously. Sandy looked back at her mother, seeking her approval one last time before leaving. Her mom nodded to the cub, and thus, her journey began.

Sandy walked along with no haste. She had yet to notice any difference from the jungle on any other day. She passed the same vine-covered tree trunks that she had passed by a million times before. The cub thought of her mother's bravery. How she longed to have that same majestic presence. Her mother seemed to her, like royalty.

The young tiger was listening to the sound that her own paws were making as they impacted the dirt. Her sharpened senses were constantly searching for anything out of the ordinary. There was only stillness. Maybe she should be the one sneaking around, she thought.

It was then that a strange call rang out from the distance. Sandy had no clue what sort of animal could produce such a sound. It seemed to pierce through the air, like a fang. Then a similar noise radiated from a different location. The sounds were communicating with one another.

The young tiger sat for a moment, listening to the bizarre jungle music. Her imagination began to run away with her, as she fantasized about the creature on the other end of that sound. Her pulse quickened, and she was filled with dread for a moment before remembering her own mother's words about bravery.

Another shrill noise echoed through the canopy above her. She padded over to the tree that seemed to hold the source of the new noise. She called to the top, asking to meet whoever was making such an ear-piercing commotion.

She was met with only silence. Sandy believed that she had scared the creature away. She did not hear the ninja-like animal dropping to the ground behind her. The young tiger felt a light tapping on her shoulder blade.

She turned to see the most interesting thing! There, before her, sat a monkey. Sandy had heard about these but had never seen one. What a curious beast! It was small and gray with lanky arms and legs and a giant tail. Somehow, the monkey had moved all around her without making a single sound.

"You are magnificent! I have never seen a monkey before. How do you move with such speed?" The tiger cub asked, marveling at the animal. The monkey seemed to be flattered by her remarks. The animal bounded around, doing flips in the air, showing off its skills to the young tiger.

"I have never seen a tiger before. I am not very old, but I can do more tricks than anyone else in my family. You did not even hear me landing behind you, huh? That is my specialty. I am so sneaky. I can sneak up on anyone!" Said the monkey.

"Yes! Your tricks are amazing! Are all animals in the jungle-like you?" Asked Sandy. The young tiger sat down in front of her new friend.

"Some of them are! There are so many interesting creatures in the jungle. You should know that, though. You live here, right?" Asked the monkey.

"I do, but I have never seen a soul. My mom is a big tiger. When she walks around, everyone

hides. Even the birds, whatever those are!"
Sandy said.

"You don't know about birds? We have some
of the most amazing and beautiful birds! I
must take you to see some of them. You will
not believe your eyes," said the monkey. "They
fly!"

"I would love to meet as many animals as
possible. I promise that I don't want to eat
anyone. I just want friends," said Sandy.

"Well, you came to the right place. You can
start with me! My name is Hank," said the
small monkey. "You can follow me, and I will
show you where some of the other animals
live, as long as you promise never to ever hunt
in these areas. Deal?"

"Deal," said the young tiger. With that, the
pair were off. Sandy was venturing away from

her trusted path, which made her a little nervous. She was so anxious to see what other oddities the jungle had to offer, so she did not complain.

The friends jumped over logs and roots. They dashed through thick brush and ducked beneath limbs. They ran for what seemed like an eternity before the monkey began to slow down.

"You have to watch your step here, there are pits of quicksand, and you will sink if you aren't careful," said the monkey.

"I have heard of those; I will be cautious," said the tiger cub.

Slowly, the air advanced upon a clearing. The sound of running water echoed through the trees, a dull roar. When Sandy was finally able to make out what lay beyond the trees, she was taken aback. Before her, it was a paradise.

There was a rocky cliffside with a waterfall that tumbled from grooves at the top. The liquid found itself spilled into a spring at the bottom of the forest floor. There were odd-looking animals standing all along the water's edge—so many interesting shapes and colors.

Hank had brought Sandy to a small oasis, deep within the jungle. There was something tranquil about the scene before the young tiger. There was harmony among creatures that she had never ever witnessed before. She slowly made her way over to the waiting pool.

The other animals stopped and stared in horror as the tiny predator drank from the spring. Sandy shook the excess water from her face, and Hank joined her side. The monkey's actions seemed to calm the nerves of the other creatures. They went right back to their conversations.

The most amazing creature dropped from the sky to join the tiger and the monkey. Hank told Sandy that the animal was a bird, called a toucan. It had a small black body with a white face and a giant orange beak. Its beak was so much larger than its head.

Hank introduced Sandy to all of the various animals standing by the spring. There were sloths and parrots and various other creatures that the young tiger had only ever dreamed of. So many monkeys made their way around the pool; each of them looked different from the last.

Sandy was quite sad when it was time to leave all her new friends. She and Hank rushed back through the brush, from which they had come.

The sun was beginning to set, and visibility was waning.

The young tiger suddenly found herself stuck in the ground. She quickly realized that she had walked right into a patch of quicksand. She began to scream for help as her heart beat faster. There was no way her mother would hear her; she was too far out.

Hank rushed away. Sandy hoped that this was not his plan the entire time. She struggled to keep her front paws above the sinking sand. The young tiger was losing hope when Hank finally returned, out of breath. Every animal from the spring joined behind him.

Without words, the larger monkeys sprung into action. One wrapped a vine around the tiger cub and began to pull. The rest of the animals helped where they could. The toucan grabbed a bit of her fur and tried to raise the cub that way; Sandy wasn't thrilled with that one.

The largest of the apes simply leaned over the pit and grasped the small tiger by the paws. He pulled as hard as he could, and finally, she could feel her body releasing from the sticky pit. Sandy was shaken up and ready to go home, but she was also grateful. She would not have changed a moment from her day, even if she could. She learned about harmony and all the different types of beauty.

There were so many lovely and talented animals out there. While she loved her stripes, she realized that they were not the only wonderful trait. You could be gray and agile or large and imposing or beautiful and neon. You could even be a bird, with a huge bill, whatever that was.

Conclusion

Thank you for making it through to the end of the best *Bedtime Stories for Kids*. I hope that this book has allowed you many precious moments with your child. Imagination is one of the most romantic aspects of our youth. Through feeding this creativity, we can allow for both bonding and learning. Your little one will remember the nights that they spent by your side, with a good story, for the rest of their lives.

Reading can be such a fundamental way to teach your little one. Each of these stories was written to pass along lessons that you are already working to instill in your child's mind. Relatable animal characters take on a laundry list of tasks that will sweep you away on some fantastic journeys.

Bedtime stories are also the most tried and tested method to help establish a nighttime routine. When you are ready for your child to go to bed, dim the lights and read a story. You will be both creating memories and establishing a cue that signals it's time to wind down. Relax as you drift off to faraway places, right alongside your little one.

You can control the content that your child consumes, and it will always work to make sure even the most chaotic of days end with an easy night. Thank you again for allowing me to take part in this bonding experience between you and your little one. Additionally, if you and your child enjoyed this book, please take a moment to leave a review on Amazon.

Printed in Great Britain
by Amazon

33143815R00126